Readers love
MIA KERICK

Us Three

"It is a highly entertaining story, with some great characters, and a truly lovely romance between the three of them."

—Love Bytes

"This is a must read, guys, especially if you're looking for a story about finding true love in the oddest of places and not only standing up for yourself, but what is right and the people you love."

—MM Good Book Reviews

The Red Sheet

"This book had me from the word go. One of the best Young Adult books I've read."

—The Tipsy Bibliophile

"*The Red Sheet* had me in awe from beginning to end. Honestly, I don't feel worthy to review it; I just hope I can do it justice."

—Prism Book Alliance

Not Broken, Just Bent

"I completely loved watching these boys grow up together."

—The Novel Approach

"Poignancy can't begin to describe this breathtaking story of two best friends."

—Twlib Reviews

By MIA KERICK

Intervention
My Crunchy Life
Not Broken, Just Bent
The Red Sheet
With Raine O'Tierney: Sound of Silence

ONE VOICE
Us Three

Published by HARMONY INK PRESS
www.harmonyinkpress.com

MIA KERICK

MY CRUNCHY LIFE

Harmony Ink

Published by

HARMONY INK PRESS

5032 Capital Circle SW, Suite 2, PMB# 279, Tallahassee, FL 32305-7886 USA
publisher@harmonyinkpress.com • harmonyinkpress.com

My Crunchy Life
© 2018 Mia Kerick.

Cover Art
© 2018 Aaron Anderson.
aaronbydesign55@gmail.com
Cover content is for illustrative purposes only and any person depicted on the cover is a model.

Trade Paperback ISBN: 978-1-64080-393-0
Digital ISBN: 978-1-64080-392-3
Library of Congress Control Number: 2017915320
Trade Paperback published June 2018
v. 1.0

Printed in the United States of America
∞
This paper meets the requirements of
ANSI/NISO Z39.48-1992 (Permanence of Paper).

To Wren and Lin—
many thanks for sharing your experiences with me.
Your openness helped me approach this story
with further authenticity.

CHAPTER 1—FRIDAY

Julian, 4:00 p.m.

ON MY first day back to school after the incident, Sydney Harper, a junior from the right side of the tracks, cut me off in the hallway by the gym and got up in my face. "You didn't really wanna die. My mother said it was just some kind of pathetic cry for help." Having made her point, she spun around on her Ugg-booted nonheel and headed for the girls' locker room.

Then in precalc, some guy I barely knew poked me hard in the back with a Sharpie marker, and I was the lucky recipient of another dose of compassion. "You just *crave* attention, don't you, girly-boy?"

Maybe, on some level, they were both right.

But on that night in October when I decided my best move in life would be to wash down the last of the Extra Strength Tylenol in our medicine cabinet with a bottle of Citrus Cooler Gatorade, I knew I couldn't lose, however it turned out. The alternative to my clever plan to get some attention, and maybe even a measure of help, was that I'd fall asleep and never wake up—which, in my opinion, served just fine as Plan B.

If nobody heard my "cry for help" and I checked out, we'd probably all be better off. No real harm done... except to Mama. But the freaking UPS man heard my "pathetic cry," or more accurately saw my apparently lifeless torso hanging from the tree house in the side yard, and saved me.

"How was school today, Julian?"

And so here I am at my weekly ER-recommended therapy session, my fine ass planted on a beige couch in a beige room with beige curtains and a beige scatter rug, spilling my rainbow guts to Dr. Evelyn, the local shrink for disturbed transgender teens. As it turns

1

out, there *are* a few other kids like me scattered randomly around Crestdale… born into the wrong damned body, and for that crime, tortured every day by family and "friends" and church people and popular girls and dudes we don't know from Adam while we're trying to learn advanced math.

"School sucked, as usual. On the bright side, it's comforting to know some things can be depended on." I tilt my "girly-boy" head and present Dr. E with my best "eat shit and die" grin.

She tosses her blonde cheerleader curls and laughs, even though I'm pretty sure she knows I'm not joking.

"Well, it *did* suck."

"Why don't you tell me what happened?"

"Okay… and remember, *you* asked. So, let's see… I was late to first period because Mama forgot to wake me up, and to make matters worse, the city bus was running behind schedule. When I finally made it to school, I got harassed by the vice principal because I'm wearing leggings and my shirt doesn't cover my stupid butt. Every single last boy in my PE class refused to be my partner, 'cause who wants to hold steady the dangling end of a 'fag's' climbing rope?" I pause momentarily to examine a jagged fingernail. "According to the dudes in my gym class, only somebody who wants an STD. And since I left my makeup bag on my bed in the frenzied morning rush, I had no powder to do touch-ups, so my face is as greasy as Colonel Sanders's crispiest chicken breast. Don't you like the way the suckage of my day came full circle, right back to my late start?"

Dr. Evelyn nods. I respect that she isn't glaring at me, or maybe rolling her eyes dramatically, because, shit, *my eyes* would be. Nope, the lady looks at me with no real expression I can make out, and bobs her head periodically, like anyone paid to be a good listener should. "And now, here you are."

"Color me thrilled." For the second time, I smile widely and then allow my eyeballs to explore the upper recesses of their sockets. Maybe Dr. Evelyn can keep her eyes from rolling, but I can't.

"I strongly suggest you write your experiences in your Transition Journal, Julian."

I have no problem with the world addressing me as Julian. In fact, I insist upon it, even with those like Dr. E, who know that, inside, I'm actually a girl. I want to be called Julian until the day I begin to live as one. I roll my eyes one more time. "Right."

"Do you know what I think you need at this point?"

I shrug and then mumble, "No, but I'm sure you're gonna tell me."

"You need to join some clubs at school… maybe the Spanish Club or Amnesty International? The more kids who get to know you in a structured social setting where there are some rules and you feel safe, the better it will be. Because you really *are* a very likable person."

"I'm already involved in more clubs than you can shake a stick at." I stop bitching for a second as I picture preppy Dr. Evelyn shaking a stick, but it morphs into a tennis racket and the image loses its power. "And if Anna and Kandy aren't also members, I sit in the corner alone." Not to be argumentative, but this is fact. Chiseled in stone. And unlikely to change over the course of my high school career.

"The other kids just don't know you well enough—if you're friendly and reach out to them, they *will* respond to you."

Yeah, they'll *respond* to me with a punch in the nose. "Try telling that to 99.9 percent of Crestdale High School students, who think gender dysphoria is contagious."

Dr. Evelyn continues as if I never said a word. "Your mother and the doctors at the Children's Gender Center think you've made enough progress to start HRT. That's going to mean big changes in your body. I think it will be best if you expand your social base before that happens."

"Expand my *social wha'*?" I know what she means, but I still play dumb just because I can.

"You need to develop additional support systems. Maybe you should join a community action group of some sort that meets *outside* the school walls—a welcoming blend of teens and adults."

"Or maybe not… maybe I'll just live out my life in lonely isolation. 'Cause, Doc, clubs don't mean friends."

It's as if I never voiced my protest. "And I know just the group.... It's a human rights activism organization, and will be a perfect fit for you."

I roll my eyes again, wondering if Dr. Evelyn has me confused with someone who cares.

Julian, 4:45 p.m.

BEFORE I leave my counseling session, Dr. Evelyn calls me over to her desk and scribbles down an address on the back of her business card. "This is where the Rights for Every Human Organization gets together. There's a meeting tonight at eight." She holds out the card and looks at me sternly. "You want life to be fair to you, Julian? Then do something about it."

I don't laugh in her face, about which I'm proud. I snatch the card, and to make a long story short, I'm currently conjuring up an outfit with a free-spirited, human rights flair. So, apparently, I'm going.

When I go somewhere new, I tend to be more conservative in how I dress. In other words, I don't drag out the feather boa and the glitter tube top and the stage makeup so I can make a shockingly femme grand entrance. But I don't throw on gray sweatpants with food stains and a Bud Light T-shirt, either. My clothing tonight should suggest that I'm in touch with my feminine self, but not scream that I *am* my feminine self. I must walk a very fine line here.

For a little while longer.

Kale, 6:30 p.m.

"I NEED a cause." *SocialActivism.com* sounds like as good a place to start as any, so I press Enter on my new Mac computer. Dad got it for me a couple months ago when he found out his nephew, Hughie, was stuck using the computer at the Crestdale Town Library to do all of his research projects for school. Since Hughie didn't have a computer of his own, his cool uncle Sam offered him the PC I'd had since middle school and replaced mine with a Mac. No complaints. Win-win all around.

My brosin—by *my* definition, a person who is midpoint between an irritating brother and an annoying cousin—Hughie, looks over at me from where he's sprawled, belly down, on the matching twin bed parallel to my own. Mom and Dad have been referring to it more and more lately as "Hughie's bed" because he sleeps in it a lot. I still call it "the spare bed in my room."

"You need a *what?*" he asks.

"All legit hippies have worthy causes. Take John Lennon. He was all about world peace. And Bob Dylan, who gave the protest song a whole new sound." I glance at Hughie, who is gawking at me, mouth wide open. "Shut your mouth, Hughie—and then there's Jerry Garcia, with his psychedelic optimism." I bookmark the activism website I'm poring over, suddenly distracted by the realization that I need to put more Grateful Dead tunes on my iPhone.

"Even Charles Manson was a hippy with a cause," Hughie says with a smugness I find maddening. "He called his purpose *helter skelter.*"

Sometimes the kid shocks me. Just when I think he hasn't got a clue, he comes out with something relevant. "Yeah… that's what I'm talking about, dude."

Hughie turns his attention back to his new/my old computer, on which he's typing faster than I thought humanly possible. He's one of the smartest kids in Crestdale High School's junior class, but he sure doesn't wear it well.

Geek alert, you know?

I keep my distance from him at school for obvious reasons. "I saw a sign at the coffee shop downtown for this local group called the Rights for Every Human Organization. It meets tonight in the Community House at eight o'clock. I'm going to ask Dad if I can use his car so I can go. I think I'm gonna find my cause there."

"I thought your cause was 'animals are friends, not food.'"

I get up off my bed and, tucking my T-shirt into my jeans, tell him, "I'm capable of multitasking."

"Are you actually *tucking your shirt in?*"

"I want to make a good impression."

"They are *human rights* activists. You are a *human being*—they'll love you. They'll probably even hug you."

I ignore his sarcasm and dish out some of my own. "Aren't you gonna wish me luck?" It feels good to throw a little shade back at him.

Hughie pushes a pillow under his chin. "You don't need me to wish you luck in being accepted by a *human rights group*. After all, you walk upright, use tools to get food, participate in social networks, and *claim* to have a large brain."

Sure in the knowledge that my brain is of a respectable size, I smirk as I walk out the doorway into the hall. "I'll fill you in on what you missed in the morning."

Kale, 8:00 p.m.

"WE GATHER tonight in the spirit of love and selflessness, and with the solemn hope that our efforts to serve the community will be sufficient to keep hope alive for those who struggle to obtain the rights inherent to all human beings."

Thanks to plenty of less-than-friendly reminders at school, I know that in profile, I resemble a mushroom. All I can say is that it's a dreadlocks thing.

Side note Dreadlocks 1A: Dreads are new to me as I only created them three months ago and I haven't fully figured out how they work. To get them started, I followed the directions on wikiHow with the care I would give to brain surgery, if, of course, I was a brain surgeon and not a sixteen-year-old wannabe-hippie. To finish the dreads on the back of my head, I had to enlist Hughie's help. Backcombing and twisting the long hair there was close to impossible for me to accomplish on my own, and I didn't want the final result to appear messy or uneven. In any case, I just recently removed the elastics that held my dreads in place at the scalp and the tips. So I'm no longer a total dreadlocks newbie.

"Now let's join hands and bond over our common concern—ridding the world of all forms of discrimination." The woman leading the prayer—Judy, according to her name tag—is short and stocky with long, frizzy red hair tied back into a humongous ponytail and decorated with a large purple velvet bow. I'd call her style "pastel flowered polyester pantsuit" featuring the comfy-elastic-waistband, but nobody asked for my opinion.

And not that all this talk about human rights isn't stimulating, but my mind returns to its previous track, because that's who I am.

Side note Dreadlocks 1B: I'd researched the whole "creating dreadlocks process" quite thoroughly before I'd attempted it on my own shoulder-length blond hair, fearing that if I messed up, I'd be forced to shave the knots from my head, and who's ever heard of a bald hippie? Over the past few months, I've learned dreads are not as carefree as one might think. They require time and attention, particularly because I don't care to smell like a wet dog, which can happen if you try to create dreads in damp hair, or if you go to sleep on a wet dreaded head.

Wet Dreaded Head would be a spectacular name for an indie rock band. Or a scented candle. Just saying.

Side note Dreadlocks 1C: Then there's special soap, baking soda scalp scrubs, oil and water spritzes (*not* vegetable oil, unless you like the idea of a rancid-smelling head, which I don't), and the application of wax to consider. It seems to me that free-spirited hippies should have figured out a way to spend less time and effort on hair care.

"Since we have a new member present tonight, I think it would be beneficial to reintroduce ourselves and the personal goals and commitments that have drawn us to the Rights for Every Human Organization." I'm gripping the sweaty palms of two complete strangers—a heavyset balding African American man and a young woman so tall I'd have to crane my neck to see her face. But I don't. I just stare straight ahead, my hands completely engulfed in their larger, moister ones.

Side note Dreadlocks 2: *Back to my resemblance to a mushroom....* The mushroom effect comes as a result of my basic need to see. Somehow, my stubborn dreads seem inclined to grow forward over my eyes, thus it is necessary to secure them in a ponytail on top of my head to get them out of my face. So picture this: my body is the pale slim stock of the fungi, my hair is the mushroom's flaring whitish cap.

"I'll start, Judy," offers an old lady standing halfway across the circle from me. Her voice is stronger and sharper than her fragile body would suggest. "I'm Edna and I believe in the equality of all people, young and old. In my day I have seen many friends and relatives being treated with less dignity than they deserve as they age, and it is just—well, it's just plain old wrong!" She's become so emotional, her voice cracks. "Don't get me going on this…. but after my dear Wilbur passed on, and after seeing how he suffered in a medical system that has no appreciation for the elderly, I joined REHO to work with others to end ageism."

I nod and my fountain of dreadlocks bobs on and off my forehead. Her cause is worthy.

"I'm Billy," says the man whose sweaty palm I'm joined with on the right. "I believe we can never rest when it comes to the inhumanity of racism. 'Cause the very minute we think the struggle for equality is over, it'll again rear its ugly head, and *let me tell you*, I know it." His voice is deep and a little bit musical, and it bounces off the walls of the basement room. "*Let me tell you….*"

He's right. Again, I nod in heartfelt agreement.

"Just because somebody looks different from other people doesn't mean he or she deserves fewer rights than others." This sentiment comes from the tall woman grasping my left hand.

I want to applaud, but I fight the urge, as I'd be forced to extricate my hands from the clenching grips of Billy and the tall lady, which may not be perceived as neighborly. I'm sure, however, I've come to the right place to find my purpose.

"I'm a Muslim woman, and as such, I wear the hijab, but I'm also a person and a citizen and… and one day I got tired of being treated like I was less than human—like I was some sort of evil being—and I joined REHO to help make a change in this perception."

Next, a semi-old dude describes his son's struggle for human rights as a person with Down Syndrome and finally, a lady the same age as Mom blabs a bunch of stuff about how there's major sexism at her office.

Again, I stifle an urge to clap because these are all excellent reasons to be here. And then everybody in the circle is looking at me. Apparently it's my turn to state my lofty reasons for joining the Rights for Every Human Organization and I know very well that my reason—every self-respecting hippie needs a legit cause—isn't legitimate at all. I look around into the compassionate eyes of the REHO members and try like hell to come up with something that sounds progressive and benevolent, yet is also remotely truthful.

"I… uh… my reason for joining… is like…," I begin, my palm sweat blending with Billy's and the tall girl's. And this is when I'm saved by the bell, or at a minimum, everyone is distracted from my dumbstruck state. I watch as all the eyes that *were* fixed on me shift toward the stairs. I feel compelled to turn my head too, to learn what has caused this ass-saving diversion. I see a small, dark-haired person posing on the bottom step, hip jutted out and arms forming question marks in the air.

He glances around, yawns like he's bored, and says, "*Please* tell me this is the human rights group, 'cause I've been all over the upstairs of this godforsaken place, and the only other creatures I came across were dust bunnies." His pompous voice brings out goose bumps on my chest, which is unexpected.

Where the rest of the group has gravitated to the bottom of the stairs, I remain in the vacated circle but twist my neck so I don't miss anything. The entrance of this new person makes me feel strangely crappy about *my* reasons for coming here tonight. I'm starting to wish Hughie were standing beside me; maybe I wouldn't feel so alone. And I'm also starting to wish for that hug Hughie incorrectly predicted I'd receive.

"Welcome to the Rights for Every Human Organization. We call it REHO," Judy says as she approaches our newest member. I wonder if she'll repeat the welcoming prayer-thing she said in the beginning of the meeting. I'm not really up for that.

"Yeah, right. Thanks," the dark-haired kid replies, and then he sighs really loud.

"I'm REHO's leader, Judy, and… well, why don't you say hello to Kale, tonight's other new member, while we fetch the pillows for the meeting." She drags the new member over to me.

We take each other in as the rest of the group feverishly grabs pillows from a large closet in the back of the room and arranges them on the floor. They're humming with the happy buzz of increased membership.

"I'm Kale Oswald," I finally say, and reach out to offer my hand.

My hand is grasped exactly as my grandmother would, making it impossible to shake. "Julian Mendez." And the way he says his name makes me think he's daring me to make fun of it. "Charmed."

There's something about this kid that puts all of my senses on high alert. Maybe it's that he's very prissy, and even though it kind of works for him, I still want to get as far away from his girliness as possible.

I study Julian's clothes, trying to make sense of who he is— purple and black plaid flannel shirt, wide open at the neck with a black velvet collar peeking out from beneath, tight black stretchy pants, and combat boots. There are some Goth girls at school who dress like this. When I note a shadow of black eyeliner underneath his dark eyes I give myself the "he's Goth" nod, but when I see the gloss on his lips, I know there's more to the story than "totally emo." A drip of sweat trickles from my hairline into my right eye socket.

What is it about this kid that's messing with my mind?

I'm scared that I *wasn't* saved by the bell, after all, and that Julian's gonna ask me why I'm here at the Rights for Every Human Organization, and the lie I tell will fall flat… and I'll be exposed, like a black spider on white tile.

"So, Kale, you say you're a champion of human rights, hmm?" It's clear to me that Julian detects my discomfort. When he steps up close, his voice emits from directly beneath my left ear. "That means you're here to protect *my* human rights, even if it takes you to a place you never figured you'd go—not even in your wildest, but most certainly unoriginal, dreams."

His breath tickles my neck—or maybe I just imagine it—and I shiver. "Yeah… that's why I came here tonight." My urge is to add "dude" to the end of my sentence, but I don't want to make an assumption.

"Really." It isn't a question or a statement. It's just a word. But the way he says it is sharp enough to cut glass.

I nod for the zillionth time tonight, and about ten thousand prickles of dread pop up in my armpits, which might sound strange, but I hear it's a common response to stress.

"Really." He says it again in exactly the same way, then steps in front of me so we're standing face-to-face. I don't want to look him in the eye. I'm not sure why I feel this way, because I've got balls. So I force myself to be a man and drag my gaze up his body from the badass combat boots, to the tights, to the oversized purple plaid flannel shirt that would make even a lumberjack look like he's going dancing. And finally I focus on the important stuff: long, dark hair, freshly brushed and falling over his shoulders, even darker eyes that lift a little bit at the corners, and an "I dare you to mess with me" smirk on shiny red lips.

His lips… well, they're moving again, but I don't have a clue what he's saying because I'm too busy staring.

At. His. Lips.

Are hippie dudes supposed to get captivated by other dudes' lips?

Because this is a first for me, and not just in my brief life as a hippie. I've *never* been one to suffer with debilitating crushes on movie stars or pop singers or the high school's most popular girls. And here I am totally caught up in the lips of a dude I don't even know. Weird.

"Kale." He says my name in the same way he said "really"—it's like a word-weapon. Sharp and deadly. And I like the way it sounds, which defines messed-up. I want him to say it again. *I don't think this is a hippie thing at all. It feels like…. Oh, never mind. Not gonna go there.*

After a final glare, Julian turns and scans the hodgepodge of pillows on the floor before us. He instantly identifies the vibrant purple cushion in the very center of the room—the prince's cushion, I guess—as his, and he walks slowly to it, crosses his legs, and sinks to the floor.

After I finish drooling at the way he struts, I find my own pillow and less gracefully drop my ass onto it.

Once we're all seated around the little prince, Judy dims the lights and says, "Tonight, friends, we have the joyful addition of two human beings who have been drawn to our group in their search to make this world a fair and equitable place for all. You've met Kale, and now please say hello to Julian."

The crowd minus me—I'm still obsessing over his lips— murmurs its greeting. "Hell-ooo, Ju-li-an."

"T-tell us th-the reasons you are h-h-here p-please," urges the guy named Tom, who stutters unless he's singing—which he confided just before the start of the meeting is what had caused him to be a subject of discrimination and cruelty when he was in high school, except in chorus.

Julian lifts his chin and glares at the group around him.

"I've been told there's nothing about any one of us that makes us less than anybody else, because we've got these things called *rights*— and we're due them because we're *people*." Julian's gaze scans his spellbound audience, but he focuses in on me, maybe because I'm the only one in the group who's close to his age. "I'm here because I want to change the world for people who are LGBTQ." We're staring at each other now—it's like the most intense staring contest I've ever… lost. Yeah, I look away first.

I think he's daring me to tease him for being gay. Because he's most likely gay, based on his stated reason for joining REHO.

I find myself hoping Julian's a fan of mushrooms.

CHAPTER 2—SATURDAY

Kale, 5:00 p.m.

"READY FOR your Saturday-night wieners, boys?" My father—the one-and-only Sam Oswald, owner of the top-ranked tire dealership in the Lakes Region, *Oh, Tires!*—steps through the foot of snow on the back deck to stand by my side. Armed with his spatula, his apron commanding in big black letters EAT MY MEAT, Dad doesn't need to waft the salty, meat-scented air in my direction, as his frenzied arm waving suggests he's attempting. The odor is already clinging to his clothing, and the hot dog smell is strong enough to give me the meat sweats.

"Don't worry, I'm aware of your precious meat," I reply, repositioning my newly vegetarian nose and pushing thoughts of the strange boy I met at REHO out of the front of my mind, where he's been living since Friday night. Yup—pretty Julian has packed a few pastel plaid suitcases and moved right into my head.

"Did you just ask me, 'Where's the beef,' Kalin?" In a single smooth move, Dad winks and rubs a frozen red ear with the inside of his elbow.

"You know I like to be called Kale." I started referring to myself as Kale at the end of tenth grade, which was roughly the time it became the superfood on which my diet is based. "And no, I didn't ask where the beef is because all I have to do is follow my nose."

"Okay, then. Boys, I'm gonna go put our wieners on the coffee table," he informs us in his typical booming voice. "On a paper plate, of course. I'm *not* a Neanderthal!"

This subject is up for debate.

Dad continues, "So go grab us a bottle of ketchup and mustard and the loaf of hot dog rolls in the bread box, Hughie-boy—and the meatfest is on!"

I'm gonna starve to death before I turn seventeen.

Dinner tonight is yet another let down. Mom is at the nail salon—
eye roll—so Dad carries out the Oswald family plan for the evening
meal: grilled hot dogs, canned baked beans with little pieces of pork
mixed in, and those slimy baby carrots from a bag. But tonight they
aren't slimy; they're kind of crusty and a little bit scary in the manner
of Grandma's dry, cracked feet. I eat them anyway. *What choice do I
have?* I sigh. My poor growing body, desperate for protein, reaches
with a shaky hand for the jar of Skippy Crunchy Peanut Butter that's
been sitting on the coffee table since breakfast.

Sometimes I wish Mom would step up to the "stay-at-home
mother" plate. She was let go from her job as a real estate agent in my
freshman year, which definitely messed with her mind, and now she
has time on her hands. The thing is, Mom hasn't slowed down at all
for the past two years—she's constantly on the go. It's almost like she
still has a full-time job. But I wish she'd get that being a homemaker
is an important job too. Dad says she's dealing with the personal and
professional devastation of being fired in her own way and we need
to be patient with her.

"You *do* know what they put in hot dogs, don't you, Dad?" I
scrape the side of the peanut butter jar with my spoon.

"Why don't you tell us, son?" His voice is patronizing, and I
don't miss the way he and Hughie exchange glances. They don't need
to make the "he's crazy" finger twirl beside their heads. I know it's
what they're thinking.

"Ever hear of mechanically separated turkey?" I ask, acid in my
voice. *Gotta punch back.*

Hughie looks concerned. "I thought these hot dogs were the
pork kind, Uncle Sam—not those healthy turkey ones."

"No worries, Hughie," I spit out. "There's some cute pink
piggy ingredients in them too—snouts and stomach and spleen and
intestines and lips." I snort twice to make my point.

Hughie nods, unaffected by both the information and the
uncanny pig imitation, and takes another huge bite of his wiener,

ketchup and mustard squirting out of the corners of his mouth. I'm not even slightly tempted to indulge. *I'm not.*

"Hughie, your… uh, mother stopped by my office yesterday," Dad says, trying to sound nonchalant, which falls flat. He's *not* a subtle man.

My brosin drops his wiener on the paper plate in front of him, sending baby carrots flying in every direction. Yes, Hughie has successfully weaponized the withered baby carrots into lethal projectiles. "What did *she* want, huh?"

Dad is the lucky one who gets to deal with his younger sister's antics in childrearing, and at times like this, I can tell it's not easy for him. "Serenity wants to see you, Hugh."

"Her name is Serenity *only* at the Dance Dirty for Me Lounge. Call her Mary Pat—*that's* her real name," Hughie scoffs.

Side note: Fact check on Hughie's statement: FALSE. Last summer, Aunt Mary Pat reportedly experienced a New-Age-ish revelation, resulting in the decision that she needed to be addressed by a new name that matched her soul—her very *serene,* reborn soul. After the revelation, Aunt Mary Pat held an intervention-style family meeting at our house, in which we all sat in a candlelit circle and she explained that, in order to seize her proper place in the universe, we all had to call her Serenity, as it was the name an angel had channeled into her mind. I didn't get it then, and I don't get it now, but I call her Aunt Serenity as often as I remember.

However, my brosin's words sound like an accusation, and I see more than annoyance in his expression; he looks petrified. Although nobody knows *exactly* what goes on inside Hughie's brain, I recognize that he's about to lose his cool in his typical sideways "won't make eye contact" way.

"Well, she's your mother… and she has a right to see you." Dad seems pretty uncomfortable pushing this issue—it's as if he thinks it's his responsibility to keep Aunt Serenity happy, even more than it is to look out for Hughie. I guess Dad's used to spoiling the women in his life. He grew up spoiling his little sister, and now he indulges my mother's *and* his little sister's every whim.

"Tell her… that I said… no." Hughie's hyperventilating. Not a joke.

Where's a brown paper bag when you need one?

"Look, you don't have to spend the weekend with her, Hugh. All she wants is to meet you for lunch."

Dad and Hughie stare at each other. Their eyeball standoff that lasts for a full minute. But Dad's encouraging words are ultimately met with stony silence. Hughie withdraws into his turtle shell.

In desperation Dad looks at me. "Kalin, I thought maybe you'd go with Hugh to the Shopper's Retreat Café next Saturday at noon. You know, to meet up with Serenity."

"My name is Kale. And how did *I* get caught up in this mess?" I plunk the empty peanut butter jar down on the kitchen table. "She's *your* sister, Dad."

Ugh. I see disappointment on my father's face, and although I'm fine with disappointing him by not eating his *Meat, Glorious Meat*, I can't let him think he raised a kid with no conscience. I am, after all, a human rights activist.

"All right, all right… don't have a cow. I'll go."

Dad winks at me and says, "We're not having cow, son, we're eating mechanically separated turkey and pig snouts." He's the only one to laugh at his feeble joke. "It'll be okay, Hugh. Your cousin will be there with you to soften the blow."

Hughie stays in his turtle shell for the rest of the night. It's like he can't bounce back from the idea of coming face-to-face with his own mother.

Julian, 6:30 p.m.

MAMA IS working extra hours at Beautiful Sunset Senior Center again tonight. Excessive guilt makes it hard to swallow down my PB and J, which is dinner since I'm too lazy to cook for myself. Puberty blockers really ought to be covered by all health insurance companies, but that's not the way it is in 2015 when you've got crappy health insurance that refuses to cover any aspect of treatment for gender issues. So Mama takes on extra hours to pay for my monthly injections

16

and for all the labs and doctor's appointments we have in the city of Norwell that go with.

When I'm finally a doctor, Mama's gonna be freaking pampered. But as for *tonight,* guilt has squelched my appetite. I put my sandwich down on the plate and head for the cabinet above the stove. Mama's gonna have a hot healthy dinner when she gets home. It's the least I can do for her.

As I reach for the can of cream of mushroom soup that I figure I'll drizzle over a chicken breast, I'm reminded of Kale from REHO. He's friggin' adorable—eye-catching in the way of a tall, thin, gilled mushroom with a domed cap, making its presence known in a deep pile of manure on the grass beside a barn. And I mean this as a compliment.

But I'm not supposed to be thinking of guys *like that*. And this is not some sort of hard, fast rule set by Dr. Evelyn—it's more what I'll call a strong guideline I set for myself. I need to stay focused on presenting myself to the world with complete authenticity, and not get distracted by a crush on a boy who would most certainly further mess with my already messed-with mind. But clueless Kale, with his stubby blond dreadlocks and his naïve blue eyes, and his *complete* inability to find the right words to explain his presence at a human rights meeting, rather captivated me on Friday night.

Sitting on a high stool at the kitchen island, pouring soup on chicken in a baking dish and sipping an espresso that will make falling asleep in a few hours next to impossible, I wonder what Kale thought of me—the teenage gay boy that I'm actually not.

Like I care what he thinks. This process requires neither his approval nor his enthusiasm.

All I need from kids like Kale is a little R.E.S.P.E.C.T.

Time will tell how deep Kale's commitment to human rights goes, but my suspicion is that he was sitting dutifully on a puffy pillow at the REHO meeting so that he could have a club's name to fill in a blank space on the College Common Application.

Against my better judgment, I send off a group text to Anna and Kandy.

Julian: *Mushroom alert. If I weren't so deathly allergic, I'd indulge.*

17

Anna: *No mushrooms for you, Julian. I don't wanna have to give you mouth to mouth.*

Kandy: *Ewwww…. LOL.*

Julian: *I'm referring to a tall, thin blue-eyed mushroom with short blond dreads.*

Kandy: *What are you talking about—a mushroom boy?*

Julian: *What can I say? This kid I met reminds me of a mushroom. Too bad mushrooms make me break out in hives.*

Anna: *And you bumped into this mushroom-boy, where?*

Julian: *If you must know, I met him at a town club at the Community House.*

Anna: *You—in a town club? With all of those conservative old people? Right!*

Kandy: *Tell us another one.*

Julian: *It's a human rights group. (Counselor mandated.) Anyway, I will be returning to REHO, if for nothing more than the eye candy.*

Anna: *Thought you said the boy was a mushroom.*

Julian: *Think of him as a mushroom dipped in white chocolate.*

Kandy: *LOL. Ewwww….*

CHAPTER 3—MONDAY

Kale, 7:00 a.m.

"STEP ON it, or I will."

I *never* step on spiders I see on the sidewalk. At least, not anymore.

I never even step on spiders that get inside the house, although sometimes I'm tempted when it comes to the hairy ones—but only out of a warped sense of self-preservation.

Kill or be killed. I, however, refuse to give in to this lowly urge.

Side note: In the jumping spider family, which accounts for 13 percent of all spiders, there are varieties that can jump more than twenty-five times their body length. This little-known fact interferes with the "live and let live" attitude I try to maintain with regard to all of Mother Nature's creatures since I have entered the world of hippiehood. Still, too much knowledge *can be* a bad thing.

"Squash the dang bug. Do it on the count of three… one, two—"

"Not a chance, Hughie!" Ever since my dad rescued him from living under the Filmore Bridge, he's acted like an annoying little brother—by six days, three hours, twelve minutes, and twenty-two seconds.

Hughie steps boldly into the spider's personal space forcing me to take to my feet.

"I said *no*, and it's *my* kitchen."

He releases a loud sigh, followed by the mandatory eye roll. "We aren't ten anymore. Just stomp on the bu-u-ug, Kale." One time he told me there were lots of bugs living under the bridge and they didn't make for good roommates, but still, the conviction in his voice is lost. Now he just sounds whiny.

"And it's not a bug, Hughie. It's a spider. There's a difference," I point out.

Once I asked Mom if, when I was a little kid, I'd had some kind of a debilitating experience with a spider that could explain my current irrational fear. She'd replied, "No, unless you count the time in kindergarten that your cousin Hugh, who just so happened to be wearing a Spider-Man costume, snuck up behind you in the Halloween parade, and pulled down your pants." Mom had then proceeded to let loose with several rather unnecessary remarks about how hilarious it had been to see a miniature Darth Vader marching down Main Street, his black pleather leggings twisted around his army boots.

"Crunchy," Hughie moans, using his nickname for me, "I'll step away from the bug if you give me a couple more minutes in the bathroom before we leave."

Maybe I *am* kind of crunchy... more on that later. "The van is leaving in five minutes, with or without you, Hugh—I mean, dude," I examine my dreads in the mirror by the door. In the early morning light, they look almost invisible, calling to mind a... jellyfish. Not the look I'm going for. "Five minutes—not one second longer."

It's not every day that I have use of the minivan, since Mom has a major shopping habit. She needs the minivan to cart herself, and her towering pile of purchases and returns, to and from Waldorph's Underpriced Fashion Center, the Crestdale Comfy Home Store, Boot Straps Gently Used Clothing Boutique, and pretty much all the shops—except the pet store—at the Sinking Stone Mall. And I'm not sure why, but Dad seems cool with Mom's shopping addiction. I never hear him complaining about it. In fact, there's a magnet on our refrigerator that says "Happy Wife, Happy Life" and *he* put it there. Who am I to question their relationship? But still, sometimes I do. I thought marriage was supposed to be about give and take, but Dad just gives and gives.

I love the independence of driving to school on the days the minivan is available. When I first got my license, I was still in my Goth phase—which came between my preppy stage and my hippie conversion—so on my way to school, I always stopped at Fresh Serve Donuts down the street for my coffee fix. Now I have to drive all the way across Crestdale, to the other side of the tracks where Hughie used to live with his mother, if I want to grab an organic cup of coffee with goat milk and raw honey at the Global Village Coffee Shop on the corner of East Street and Fifth Ave.

When Hughie emerges from my bedroom, his dark curls are plastered to his head like a wavy, brown storm-trooper helmet.

"What's up with your hair, dude?"

He pushes me away from the hall mirror and examines his head, turning this way and that to see himself from different angles.

"Did you grease it down or something?" I poke the top of his head with my index finger and it comes away sticky. "Not cool." I wipe my finger on my organic cotton pants; it leaves behind an oil slick.

After turning his back to the mirror and glancing over his shoulder to get one last perspective, Hughie asks quietly, "Do you know Sydney Harper?"

I shake my head. "I haven't had the pleasure."

"Well, she told me that my curls remind her of dog turds." He turns around and looks at me directly, which doesn't happen too much. Hughie's *not* a straightforward sort of dude. "So I thought maybe if I used Aunt Kathy's hair gel, I could straighten it out some, you know, and, like, flatten it."

I shake my head, realizing that there's not going to be any organic coffee in my immediate future. "You need to get back in the shower, or at a minimum stick your head in the kitchen sink."

"Why? My hair's straight now."

"It looks like somebody cracked an egg over your head. You can't go to school like that." I sigh. "And believe me, that Sydney girl will eat you alive if you show up looking like you're ready to do battle in space."

"Huh?"

"You've got a serious case of helmet-head, dude. So just get in the shower. I'm setting the timer on my phone—you have ten minutes to degrease your hair." *Jeez.* "I'll be in the van pretending I'm sipping on organic Rainforest blend."

21

Julian, 7:10 a.m.

EVERY ONCE in a while, I dare to make a feminine fashion statement at school, which I woke up needing to do today. It would have been much easier to accomplish wearing my chunky suede booties, but since I broke a heel off the left one while speed walking home from my counseling session last Friday, I make the executive decision to go Goth. I wear black better than anybody.

As I towel dry my hair, I think about how much I've changed since the incident. The first thing I did when I was released from the hospital was change my personal style to better reflect the person I am on the inside, even though I knew it would make things harder for me at school. I actually *had* to do it in the interest of maintaining my sanity. But I hate that when I get dressed in the morning for school all I can see in my head is Sydney Harper's sneer. She should have absolutely zero to do with my clothing choices, or any other choices I make. The problem is I'm not yet detached enough to ignore her disdain, when she's clearly thinking that I look like a freaky femme in leggings.

Her voice echoes in my head:

"Mrs. Rosen, you said you wanted the boys on one side of the room and the girls on the other, but where do the she-males like Julian go?"

"Julian, you can put lipstick on a pig, but it's still a pig."

"You're in the wrong place if you're looking for RuPaul's Drag Race, *Juliana."*

As I pull on yet another carefully selected androgynous ensemble—a black-sleeved baseball shirt with a skull and crossbones on the front and torn black skinny jeans—I remind myself that high school is not a fashion show and I don't go there to receive anyone's stamp of approval. Which is a very good thing because I don't think I'd have much success if this were my goal. I go to school to get straight *A*s in the most challenging classes so that I can earn a full ride to a competitive college, and then go on to medical school, specialize in pediatric endocrinology, and take care of Mama.

By the time I get downstairs, Mama's already gone, and the guilty feeling surges like adrenaline in my veins. How long can she keep doing this—working twelve-hour shifts, five days a week? My frequent guilt-fests seriously interfere with my ability to eat, but I manage to force down a banana. Maybe I'll stop by the Global Village Coffee Shop on the corner for a caffeine infusion before I get on the school bus.

I grab my trench coat, sling my messenger bag full of books over my shoulder, and head out the door. There's just enough change jingling around in my coat pocket to buy a small cup of liquid energy at the coffee shop. As I walk down the sidewalk, though, I can't stop my brain from adventures in time travel.

After that day last fall when it all became too much for me and I decided I wanted out of this pretty little thing called life, it was clear to everybody who gave a shit that certain aspects of my existence had to change. Not only had I been suffering over bullying at school— which was par for the course in my life—but I had also become newly horrified with the changes that were starting to happen to my body. Hair growth in places I wanted to stay smooth, my muscles getting thicker and my voice deeper—I was freaking out more each day. Soon I was in a hole so deep I was sure that I'd never be able to climb out.

I think of it as my own personal hell.

As I push open the heavy glass door to the coffee shop, I notice that it's busier than usual this morning. So I get in line and ponder how I arrived at this ambiguous place in my so-called life. Becoming a technical girl requires a lot of introspection.

After everything was said and done—in other words, when I didn't kick the bucket as planned—Mama and me finally had the "big talk." I remember saying, "I only want to keep living if I can be my true self, and that means being the same girl on the outside that I am on the inside."

At first she'd come back with, "Gender is just between the ears, Jules," but she'd accepted it when I told her that changing my mind wasn't enough. I wanted to live in a body that felt like my own.

23

And so, at the Children's Gender Center in Norwell, it was decided I would receive counseling and puberty blockers. It was as if they'd proclaimed, "Let there be life…."

"Let there be life." I say it out loud, but everybody around me in line is so stoned or eclectic they don't gawk at me for talking to myself. They either shrug or nod or say something like, "Yeah, dude, let there be life."

I grin and know that I now appear about as off my rocker as the rest of the crowd in this "free to be you and me" coffee shop. But realizing I could stop time—in terms of my puberty—had been a *wow!* moment in my life. A life-changing, survival-allowing *wow!* moment.

When I'm three customers from the front of the line, I glance into the glass case of vegan bakery items. *Hmmm….*

The theory is that puberty blockers will buy me some time—by stopping all of the physical changes that occur during puberty—so I can be "sure" I want to take more permanent steps in changing my gender. Next step—Hormone Replacement Therapy. *Woot!* I don't shout aloud because there are limitations to public vocal expressions of joy, even in this bizarro coffee shop. And the joy quickly fades— my transition has a major downside, and it's always on my mind: endless work cycles for Mama to pay for it.

Sometimes the burden of guilt's almost too heavy to carry.

"Changing genders isn't free, Jules."

I sigh and place my order, investing the change in my pocket in the purchase of a whole-grain carob-chip muffin that I'll present to my mother tonight for her evening snack instead of going with my original plan for a morning caffeine infusion.

Kale, 7:15 a.m.

"SO TELL me about that girl Sydney—the one who thinks your hair is crap." I giggle because I'm such a riot. *Crap… dog turds. Hehehe.*

"She's a junior, like us. And she's what I'd call a bitter nerd." *Hmmm…* so this Sydney girl isn't a member of the beautiful crowd.

24

Incidentally, I'm proud that *my* social group circles the outside edge of the beautiful people. I've worked damned hard for this semilofty status. Poor Hughie is way down the food chain—even bitter nerds reign over him.

I nod and pull into Fresh Serve Donuts. Hughie, slumped beside me in the passenger seat, seriously looks like he could use a chocolate donut. "Is this Sydney girl in one of your classes?"

"No. She's in *all* of them. There are three of us who have almost all the same classes. Me, Sydney, and this boy who everybody says is gradually turning into a girl."

"Weird." Before I can stop myself, I think of Julian again. He's most certainly a guy but has a lot of girly stuff going on. It can't be him, though—he doesn't go to Crestdale High School.

"Sydney sure thinks so. She treats him even worse than she treats me."

As Hughie's hair dries, it slowly separates into the usual fat round curls that cover the entire back of his head. I don't think they look like dog turds at all. They look more like chocolate crullers. "In the mood for a couple of chocolate crullers and some hot chocolate, dude? My treat."

"You gonna eat something too?" I wonder if my brosin truly doesn't like to eat alone or if he wants me to serve as his food taster. Hughie has trust issues. He has never been the same since Dad rescued him from underneath that bridge.

Fresh Serve crullers are definitely not made with whole-wheat flour, and the hot chocolate is probably loaded with pesticides. But this moment calls for shared food, so I'll grab a bagel and a cup of tea, and then eat like a fruitarian for the rest of the day to make up for it.

"Sure." I wrinkle my nose. "Stay buckled, I'll go through drive-thru."

I look over at Hughie so that we can exchange a wink or a smile or *something* human to confirm that we're on the same planet, but Hughie stares straight in front of him.

Can you say "lost cause"?

Julian, 7:30 a.m.

A BANNER hangs above the main entrance to Crestdale High School. It states in bold red letters: A BULLY-FREE ZONE. Unfortunately, somebody forgot to tell Sydney and her vicious gang of nerds this vital piece of information. And it *has* crossed my mind that *I* could step up to the plate and inform her of this enlightening news myself. But seeing as I no longer have a death wish, I wisely hold back.

In any case, this morning she goes about the business of making my life hell, as is her usual morning routine.

I step up to the boys' bathroom door, refusing to look at Sydney, who is leaning on a nearby wall and eyeing me expectantly. She's been waiting for me. And I know full well that I can't beat Sydney at her game; she's way too good at it. I bet she told off the doctor who delivered her at birth.

Sydney throws her body between me and the entrance to the boys' room. "You can't go in there." My nemesis is alone this morning, as it's early and her clones have apparently not yet arrived. I'd like nothing better than to feel relieved, but I know better. She doesn't need help in achieving her wicked agenda.

"Uh, *excuse me*, Mother Nature's calling my name and I plan on answering her," I inform Sydney in my haughtiest tone, but still refuse to look her in the eye. I think it's a passive-aggressive thing. If she can't see the pain in my eyes, she won't be able to enjoy the torture so much.

Without moving out of the doorway, Sydney replies, "Just for shits and grins, tell me what name Mother Nature calls you—her *little freak?* Because you define *freak of nature.*" Hughie calls her a bitter nerd. It's a fitting label. She should get it tattooed on her lower back.

But I refuse to play this game.

I yank my mind out of the hallway, and away from Sydney's glare. I try to place my awareness in my living room... on my couch... close beside Mama where I'm safe.

"You must be in quite a quandary! Everybody knows you're a she-male, so you can't use the boys' room, because of the *she* part. It just wouldn't be right, you know? And you can't use the girls' room, because girls don't pee standing up." Sydney speaks in a loud, expressive tone, as if she's auditioning for the lead role in the spring play. Sydney wouldn't get the role, though, because she's a bitter nerd not a theater geek.

I glance around as her voice echoes off the walls and I'm relieved that we're still alone in the hallway. I've been in worse spots than this, but still, my cheeks burn and my stomach gurgles, rejecting the bacon-egg-and-cheese biscuit I just forced down in the cafeteria. "Get out of my way or… or I'll…." *Shit. I got nothing.*

Sydney lets her thirty-pound backpack slide off her shoulders and drop to the floor. She then steps forward, grabs my chest with both hands, and squeezes. I gasp, humiliated and hurting, which seems to encourage her, and she adds a little twist to the squeeze. "You're such a disgusting *thing*—you should be kicked out of school!"

The words hurt, but this time Sydney has crossed a line in her bullying—putting her hands on me is a new and disturbing tactic—and my heart starts to pound. I try to push her hands away, but she grabs my shirt and hangs on.

"I'd say you're a double A…. Sorry, Juliana, but you're gonna need a training bra."

I make the mistake of glancing at her face… and looking right into her eyes. I see so much hate and anger that, even through my fear, I find myself wondering how she got to this place. "Leave me alone," I tell her again, fighting to keep my voice from rising in pitch and volume, but it isn't easy. "Get your paws off me."

"Make me." She smiles, pleased that I squirmed.

I don't want to run off like I'm scared, because that would be the same as sending out a personal handwritten invitation to Sydney via first-class mail, asking her formally to harass me in the future. All I want is to go into the bathroom stall, brush my hair, roll on fresh lip gloss, and be alone so I can catch my breath.

"What's going on here?" A voice I know, and one I've grown to trust, comes from out of nowhere. I turn and see Kandy approaching, but for my purposes she's a rescuing knight on a white stallion. I breath a loud sigh of relief, but quickly disguise it with a cough.

At the sound of Kandy's voice, Sydney drops her hands from my chest. She steps back, makes a huffing sound and, when Kandy reaches us, rolls her eyes with a vengeance. "We're just chatting. Right, Juliana?"

Sydney doesn't seem interested in sticking around to finish what she started, probably because she knows what kind of havoc a suspension for bullying would wreak on her chances of getting into a top college. Besides, she made her point: Julian Mendez is a freak—a boy with tiny tits. She doesn't know a thing about being transgender, but she *does* know something isn't "normal" about my gender. Sydney can see that I'm not your everyday boy, but just as clearly, I'm not an average girl. So she's compelled to torture me.

I don't want to go into the bathroom anymore; there isn't a bathroom for me. And no matter what choice I make about my future gender status, I don't foresee there being a public bathroom I can use anytime soon. I sigh and say, "Let's get outta here, Kandy."

CHAPTER 4—TUESDAY

Kale, 12:30 p.m.

LUNCH IN the cafeteria… used to be so cool. When Mom lost her job freshman year, school lunch became the highlight of my day.

I've had to face the facts: school lunch is the closest thing I can get to a home-cooked meal because ever since Mom lost her job, she's lost all interest in cooking. At this point, Mom can't, or won't, cook up a casserole to save her life. She has a long list of excuses for her disinterest in the kitchen… and the grocery store… and all things related to feeding us.

Dad tells me over and over that Mom isn't obligated to cook anything because we're completely capable of feeding ourselves. He also says she's dealing with a loss and a huge life change, so I need to take a step back and let her deal with her unemployment in her own way. Whatever the case may be, chop suey and canned green beans, heated up by an adult and served to me with a side of orange Jell-O on a faded seafoam green plastic plate, was my idea of food heaven until the hippie conversion late last spring when I stopped eating everything that had a face.

Everything is different now that I'm crunchy.

Last summer, when I made the decision to move forward in my life as a hippie, I knew I had to look at every aspect of my life, from soup to nuts, so to speak. And then I had to rework things according to the hippie philosophy.

One Sunday afternoon in August, I spent hours researching the hippie way.

Side Note: The Basic Tenets of Being a Proper Hippie:
reject established institutions
reject middle class values

29

be eco friendly
eat all-natural and vegetarian
experience free love
oppose violence
embrace peace and freedom

I remember the research had been involved and exhausting, and I'd soon needed to refuel. So in my first official act as a hippie, I went to the kitchen in search of an all-natural/vegetarian snack. I found plenty of Dad's favorites, seeing as he was the one to do the grocery shopping each week: beef jerky and corn dogs, bologna and barbeque chicken wings. But there were no berries, pumpkin seeds, or bean sprouts to be found. This is when I spotted an old box of granola. I pulled it down from the top pantry shelf, dusted it off, and stuck my hand inside to grab a fist full. The contents were stale, but I was pleasantly surprised by the lightly sweet, still vaguely crunchy, whole-grain snack that I'd, until then, always considered the best part of Dad's apple crisp.

Side note: The term *crunchy* is based on the consistency of granola, but it refers to the all-natural, green mindset of the hippie.

And back in the day, before the whole "living under the bridge" incident, when Hughie still had some semblance of a sense of humor, he'd picked up on my granola obsession. Hughie was the one who first called me Crunchy, but it stuck.

Half the school calls me Crunchy now.

School lunch looks much different when you remove the chop suey from that seafoam plastic plate. Yup. All you're left with is a pathetic pile of soggy canned green beans and no orange Jell-O, because gelatin is made out of horses' hooves, or so I've heard. And I *am* a self-professed veggie-hugger, but I'm discouraged as I sit here between Jared, who is opening his packed-by-Mom gourmet lunch, and Robbie, who is consuming six pounds of "salad." I hesitate to call it salad, though, since it consists of crispy chicken, chopped egg, and macaroni on top of buttermilk ranch dressing-soaked lettuce from the cafeteria's "Good-for-you Green Stuff Salad Stand"—where each and every premade salad is sprinkled liberally with bacon bits. But seriously, green beans suck donkey balls.

"It ain't easy being green, huh, Crunchy?" Robbie is an offensive tackle on the high school football team, and he thinks he's a total riot, but he's not. He speaks between mouthfuls of bacon-coated macaroni salad.

"Shut up, Robert." According to my long-held philosophy that the best defensive move equals a strong offensive counterpunch, I choose my words carefully and deliver them decisively. "I wouldn't touch that meat salad you're inhaling with a ten-foot fork." Unfortunately, the disdain in my voice rings false. Plus, I'm drooling, which is always a dead giveaway of pure, unadulterated envy.

"So, did you go to that town club meeting last weekend, the one you were telling us about?" Jared is unwrapping what appears to be a baguette from a neatly folded sheet of wax paper. My traitorous mouth waters at the sight. I punish it with a forkful of rubbery beans.

But I can't take my eyes off the baguette. "Yeah. I went to the meeting and joined the club." *Oh jeez, there's a thick slab of sausage inside....*

"Human rights, ya said?" Robbie stabs his plastic fork into the salad and pulls it out with half of a hard-boiled egg, miraculously free of bacon bits, attached. "What a waste of a Friday night."

At the moment, I don't even give a hoot if it's a free-range chicken's organic egg. "Um, Robbie, you gonna eat that egg?"

"This egg?" He stuffs it into his pie hole.

"That's it—I've had it!" I push myself up from the narrow bench and head for the snack display by the cash register. I'm reasonably certain there's a granola bar to be had. And this is when I see those shiny red lips. "Julian?"

He glances up at me and his eyes widen, which proves that I'm not imagining him. Julian and his awesome lips are at the cash register, flashing a reduced lunch card at the kitchen lady. "Kale." I can tell he's as surprised to see me as I am to see him. "I didn't know you went to Crestdale High."

"Yeah, same here... I mean, about you. Uh-huh." Starvation has clearly addled my brain. "Yeah," I mumble again for good measure. And although he's not wearing khaki-colored hemp overalls and an

31

organic cotton T-shirt like me, I admit to myself that he looks good in the same androgynous way he did at REHO.

Crap, I'm staring at his lips again.

Mutual nods are followed by an awkward silence that I want to fill with questions—*What are you doing here? Why have I never seen you at school before? Are you a junior, like me?* But nope, there's just silence.

"So… I guess I'll see you on Friday night," Julian says, sounding bored.

"Yeah," I repeat like a loser and watch as he walks off with his tray in hand and sits alone on the end of the closest table. "Uh-huh."

I want to call after him, to say, "Hey, Julian, you don't have to sit alone." But I don't.

My mind wanders to the beginning of the REHO meeting on Friday night, when we took the somber oath.

"We gather tonight in the spirit of love and selflessness, and with the solemn hope that our efforts to serve the community will be sufficient to keep hope alive for those who struggle…."

Looks like I *was* paying attention to Judy's oath as she welcomed us to the Rights for Every Human Organization. And I was listening carefully enough to know that I just broke my vow.

Julian, 7:00 p.m.

I DON'T get home from school until after the Amnesty International meeting and two hours of volunteering as a cat-patter at the Crestdale Humane Society. I have to take the city bus home, so by the time I get here, it's almost seven.

I'm freaking exhausted, and added to that, I'm freaking starving, because I only ate three bites of the chop suey served at lunch today—it was way too bland. And then there were the green beans. Those things should be outlawed. Or maybe used as pencil erasers. In any case I didn't eat very much.

It'll be a pasta night. I make the executive decision to put a pot of water on the stove even though all I want is to crash on the couch. I pop open a jar of marinara sauce, pour it into an already-stained Tupperware bowl, and stick it in the microwave. Finally I plunk my ass down in a chair at the kitchen table, lay my head sideways on the inviting flat surface before me, and let my mind wander while I wait for the water to boil.

The reason I'm pretty much always exhausted is because my plan to be offered a full ride at a decent college requires that I study constantly and am involved in as many after-school activities as I can fit into my schedule, since I don't do sports. This is where Anna and Kandy come into the picture.

Anna and Kandy are what I call "volunteer friends." To be blunt they have *literally volunteered* to hang around with me as an act of charity and humanitarianism.

There's a story behind my volunteer friendships. In October, after the incident, word quickly spread at Crestdale High School that Julian Mendez tried to off himself in the old tree house in the side yard of his duplex. And rumor, in this case, was quite accurate. According to my volunteer friends, over the next eight or so weeks when I was out of school, there was extensive speculation as to the reasons for what I did.

Among them:
spat with secret gay lover
poor PSAT scores
cruel pants-ing prank in gym class taken too far
unable to handle inappropriate relationship with drama club director, Mr. Henley
unexpected cancellation of local stop on Barbra Streisand tour
pet kitten, "Rainbow Brite," got run over by a car

None of these hit the nail on the head, although the bullying *was* getting out of control. I have never had a gay lover seeing as I'm *not gay*. I expect to be nominated as a National Merit Scholarship Finalist thanks to my high PSAT scores; Mr. Henley doesn't know I'm alive; Barbra is not on tour; I live in a no-pets-allowed apartment.

Mama and I, with the help of Dr. Evelyn, got to the root of my problem: I am a girl living in a boy's body. Over the summer before the incident, my boy's body had started turning into a man's body, which horrified me. I wanted boobs not a mustache, for God's sake.

Sure, the bullying, the loneliness, and being a social pariah took their toll on me. But I can and always could take it; I'm strong. After the incident, I was much more fragile than ever before. I hate the thought of it, but I was like a glass doll—nobody careless could handle me. So before I returned to school, Mrs. Donovan, a guidance counselor at Crestdale High School, recruited volunteers from Kids Help Kids Antibullying Club to walk with me from class to class, sit next to me at club meetings, and call me at night so I didn't feel like a Martian living in isolation on the unfriendly planet Earth. Hence, my two volunteer "BFFs," Anna and Kandy.

I wonder if they'll put me down as a volunteer activity on their college applications.

I like to think we're *real* friends now.

The sound of water bubbling in the pot, not to mention my growling stomach, encourages me to get up, grab the box of bow tie noodles, and dump it. After setting the timer and stirring, I head out to the living room for twelve minutes of pure *me time.*

The couch beckons, so I flop down on my back and stare at the ceiling. I see a new water stain directly above me. It's in the distinctive shape of a mushroom. And where I should be rushing up the stairs of our duplex to see if there's a leak in the toilet, I instead let my mind wander to a subject I find more enticing. More interesting.

More painful.

I was pretty floored to learn that Kale from REHO also attends Crestdale High School. When the kids from the middle school on the right side of the tracks joined with the kids from the one on the wrong side at the start of freshman year, our graduating class became very large. I must have passed by Kale a hundred times, in the halls and in the cafeteria, but was too caught up in my own drama to take notice.

Today he noticed me first. He said my name and then I said his. And that was where it began and ended. I'm a fool for that split second where I let myself think he was going to invite me to sit with him.

Honestly, I never actually believed he'd sacrifice his social standing to sit with me. I'm too world-weary to think I might finally have found a nonvolunteer friend.

Kale, 10:00 p.m.

"We gather tonight in the spirit of love and selflessness, and with the solemn hope that our efforts to serve the community will be sufficient to keep hope alive for those who struggle to obtain rights inherent to all human beings."

Judy's oath. Ever since I got in bed, it's been running across the bottom of my mind like ticker tape. Seriously annoying ticker tape.

I think it might be guilt that's causing me to obsess over the REHO oath. Guilt that I've been a member of a human rights group for roughly a week and I've already failed at its most fundamental requirement.

"Will you cut it out with the heavy sighing, Kale? I can't sleep."

"Shut up, Hughie. Remember, it's *my* room."

"I'll shut up when you do."

Maybe I *wanted* to sit with Julian today at lunch. Maybe I wanted to sit down and ask him why he joined REHO in the first place and why he wears lipstick and eyeliner and why he was eating all by himself. But I looked the other way at REHO's spirit of love and selflessness, and that fact gets to me.

And then there's the *minor* issue of *Hello, world! Am I gay*?

Ugh. So instead of facing the tough stuff, I skulked back to the security of my supposed friends and let Julian's hope for the friendship he needs die.

"You are physically unable to stop sighing. I'm sleeping on the couch." Hughie grabs his pillow and comforter and stomps from the room.

"Sleep tight." I close my eyes and sigh one last time, but the ticker tape keeps running.

CHAPTER 5—WEDNESDAY

Julian, 10:30 a.m.

THERE ARE two kids who are in all of my classes—every last one. And we're the three students who are already competing for class valedictorian, salutatorian, and the untitled and clearly less desirable position of number three.

First, there's the nastiest girl in the grade, Sydney Harper. Calling her a *mean girl* is so clichéd, and maybe it isn't an exact fit, because she isn't blonde and popular and pretty, and she's definitely not a cheerleader, but she *is* crazy mean.

And *if the cliché fits....*

Then there's Hughie Oswald, who is just plain shifty. He never looks anybody straight in the eye—not students or teachers or custodial staff—so, I figure, he's got to be hiding something. And Hughie doesn't seem like your average smart kid—nothing about him fits the "I have far-reaching knowledge of Star Wars so go ahead and quiz me" nerd stereotype *or* the "destined for Yale golden boy" preppy image. He seems like a potential sociopath who couldn't possibly have his academic act together, but does.

Number three in this messed-up trio of brainiacs is me, the "snarky gay boy" who is actually a straight girl living inside the wrong body.

"You're drooling at my shoes, aren't you, girly-boy?" Sydney never misses an opportunity to give me hell. "We both know you want them." I sincerely hope she doesn't throw one at me.

"Yeah, girly-boy." Emma can be counted on to echo Sydney's sentiments. I firmly believe she would echo them with her dying breath.

And then comes Jory. She's number three on the Sydney Harper-clone-slur-delivery totem pole. "Admit it, she-he."

Since only two of her female henchwomen are smart enough to be in AP US History class, the heckling is minimal. And yes, Sydney's shoes rock—*who wouldn't want purple platform oxfords*—but that's beside the point. She's trying to distract me from my work.

"And Oswald, is that Hello Kitty Superman shirt supposed to be amusing? Because it's not."

"Seriously lame T-shirt," Emma says.

"Like, what were you thinking when you got dressed this morning, Hubie?" Jory asks.

Hughie's face flushes as cherry red as his shirt. Nonetheless, he never lifts his eyes from his textbook.

"You wear that stupid shirt so often—do you think it's the Crestdale High School uniform or something? News flash, Hubie! You're free to wear anything you want… so why don't you go for a Wonder Woman T-shirt tomorrow?" Sydney flashes her evil white smile.

"A Hello Kitty Wonder Woman T-shirt!" Emma adds.

"Superheroes are losers! LOL, Sydney!" Jory chimes in.

Hughie and I are Sydney's favorite victims. We're easy targets for a variety of reasons, but an added bonus is that if she succeeds in getting under our skin enough to cause one of us to have a nervous breakdown and thus flunk out of or quit school, she is a step closer to valedictorian.

This is serious business to Sydney. She has no idea that her consistent record of cruelty has likely already won her one of the top two spots in Crestdale High's class ranking. The "snarky gay boy" probably won't be around to see graduation.

"Okay, kids. I would like to see you partner up for mock presidential interviews, which will be our next major project. You have all done your research on FDR, now you need to prepare interview questions with your partner," Mr. Trainer instructs the class, interrupting Sydney's efforts in psychological warfare.

Sydney turns her back to her clones and faces me. "I'll work with *you*, Juliana." She may be cruel, but she's also smart. She knows her best chance at an A+ is with Hughie or me. It's hard to believe that she'd try to be my partner after how she acted yesterday morning outside the boys' room, but I guess an A+ is an A+.

"Think again, Harper. Hughie and I are already working together."
He looks at me, which is a rare event to say the least. *What the hell?* is in
his eyes because this is news to him. He usually insists on working alone.

Switching on a dime, Sydney counters with, "Hugh, you know
you'll do better if you work with me. Mr. Trainer *loves* me." She
bats her eyelashes but it's lost on Hughie because, naturally, he isn't
looking at her. "Get over here and sit down."

"I told you that Hugh already said he'd be my partner." Although
I rarely touch people at school, seeing as they think they could catch my
gender confusion, I grab the kid by his wrist and pull. And Hughie doesn't
shake me off. He comes my way without even a hint of resistance.

"What—are you gay too, Hubie? I should've known." She takes
a few seconds to glare at him. "Sir Dog-turd-hair and Lady Juliana,
you two will regret your stupid decision, even if you do make a
rather… interesting… couple." I wait for the sound of cackling, but
surprisingly there is none. We watch as she informs Emma that she
will be pairing up with Jory, so *get lost.*

"What a bitch," I say, unable to refrain. "I keep wondering when
her bad karma is gonna catch up to her."

For approximately the third time this semester, Hughie Oswald
lifts his eyes from the floor and he looks at me. "If anybody asks, *you*
said it; *I* didn't. But you're right—she's a total b-word."

He talks too! I pat myself on the back, literally. I got water from
a rock. "Okay, you wanna be FDR?"

"You can be him and I'll ask the questions." I'm not surprised
by his answer; Hughie hates the limelight. "Think Sydney's gonna
grill us and eat us for lunch?"

Kale, 3:00 p.m.

STANDING IN the hallway at the junction of the science and mathematics
corridors, I debate whether I should walk left, toward the Gay-Straight
Alliance meeting, or right, toward the buses and home and freedom.

I should really go to the Gay-Straight Alliance meeting today because I need the names of a few clubs to fill in all of those blank spaces on my future college applications. More importantly, back when I first became a hippie, I told myself that GSA was a club I really ought to join because it reinforces two of the Basic Tenets of Being a Proper Hippie: rejecting established institutions and embracing peace and freedom. The thing is, there are two really good reasons why I *don't* want to go.

Number one is Julian's lips. Before meeting Julian Mendez and his captivating lips at REHO, the Crestdale High GSA was just a club I figured I ought to join. Now, I think it might be an alliance I really need, seeing as I've been thinking about another boy's lips far too much for my own comfort. And I don't know a sixteen-year-old guy who is eager to head down the "Am I gay?" path.

It shouldn't matter to me if I'm gay, straight, or if I'm what any of the other letters in LGBTQIA stands for. I'm a free-spirited and open-minded human rights activist. Going to this meeting is just an example of global citizen, free-loving me being me. But it isn't that simple at all. Maybe I don't want to take a closer look at my sexuality, which could very possibly happen at a Gay-Straight Alliance meeting.

Second, by the end of every single school day since I was in kindergarten, I've craved the mental freedom that comes with the 3:00 p.m. bell. I've been told what to think about for the past eight hours, and now I want to go home and dwell on the stuff I'm interested in— about how far a spider can jump and what the best thing was *before* sliced bread. And if man is evolved from apes, why do we still have apes? Stuff like that.

But I haven't been to a meeting since the second week of school, and if I want to be able to write GSA on my college applications.... I reluctantly head left, toward the science wing.

Unfortunately, I arrive late and the discussion is well under way, so I sneak into the classroom and sit in the back row. There are about twenty kids in the room, and addressing the group in front by the white board is the GSA staff leader, Ms. Valencia. She's the biology teacher you get if you're lucky with scheduling. And rumor has it she's a lesbian. Just saying.

"We need to discuss inclusion and exclusion in the school society, folks." Ms. Valencia sends a meaningful glance to the group. She even takes a second to look directly at me and smile. "Without a feeling of inclusion here at Crestdale High School, it cannot be a safe place for every student, and that's not acceptable. So my proposal is that we set up a Respect Week with activities offered during the three lunch periods, and we end it with an ice cream social. Rainbow sherbet, right guys?"

Anna Morris, a girl so sweet it makes my teeth ache, raises her hand. "Maybe we could do it on the week of Valentine's Day, because it's a way of showing love for our fellow students."

"That's an excellent idea, Anna. How do the rest of you feel about that?"

The group murmurs its assent.

"I think we should make an effort to visibly define respect," someone suggests.

"It would be better if we could show people the shit that makes LGBTQ kids feel disrespected." *This* voice, I recognize. In fact, I can almost *see* the shiny red lips moving…. I lean forward so I can confirm it's Julian Mendez who spoke.

"I think that would work really well, Julian. Before we leave today, I'd like to come together to brainstorm ways we can demonstrate the pain of *disrespect* to the student body on Respect Week." Ms. Valencia lifts a notecard off the teacher's desk and glances at it. "I think it's time we break into small groups for discussion. The topic of discussion is this: recall a time when you felt especially included and respected at Crestdale High School. And then recall a time when you felt especially excluded and disrespected here. Choose one answer for each question per group and we will then come together and share."

The students start to split up into small groups. I look around for a group to join, but Ms. Valencia says, "Hey, Kale, welcome back to the Gay-Straight Alliance. Come on over here. Anna, Kandy, and Julian could use a fourth member in their group."

As obedient as a nonhippie, I grab my backpack and coat from the back of the chair and head toward the front of the room.

"Kale, are you stalking me?" Julian asks with such a straight face that I think he's serious, and I start to deny it. "Relax, I'm joking. It's just that since we met at the human rights group, we keep on bumping into each other. But, on the bright side, my stalking accusation can be your example of when you felt most *disrespected* at school."

Anna and Kandy laugh, so I do too.

As there isn't an available desk nearby, I make myself comfortable on the counter beside the window and look down at my group. "Don't worry, I've had worse things happen to me here at Crestdale High School."

"Give us the dirt, Kale." Word is that Kandy is a regular saint, and actually is rumored to have risked her own life by saving a little boy from drowning on a church outing last summer at the town beach. She adjusts her glasses and fixes her dark eyes on me.

"I guess it's just a feeling I get sometimes, not a single situation." I'm not sure how comfortable I am with spilling my soul to these relative strangers. But it looks like I've joined the group, so I might as well participate.

"We're listening." Anna reaches out and touches my knee, which is a pretty gutsy move—not to mention sort of sappy—but it serves its purpose and I feel supported.

"Well, I think it's just...." I dig deep, which isn't the easiest thing in the world to do, and continue. "It's just a feeling I get every once in a while... that I'm nobody around here. I'm not an academic superstar, and I'm not a jock. And if you heard me sing, you'd know I'd never be welcome in the musical theater program."

They laugh again and I feel good. Included. Respected.

"I feel really excluded at the school dances. Me and Kandy don't even go to them anymore." I look at Anna and she's staring at Kandy, as if for courage. "I've been to twenty-five dances since middle school, and, except for Kandy, nobody has ever asked me to dance. Even the girls who are supposed to be my friends make these tight circles with their bodies and won't let me in."

I fight the urge to shout, "Been there; done that!"

Julian is the one to console her. "If I went to dances, *I'd* dance with you, Anna. But if I went to dances, I'd get beat up in the boys' bathroom. Bathrooms are *not* friendly places for people like me."

The girls look at him and frown, but it's as if Julian's words reach into my chest, grab my heart, and wring it out like a yellow kitchen sponge. I never thought much about how it feels to be scared of getting beat up at school just for being who I am.

"But you should see me dance—I got the rhythm in me!" Julian stands up and swings his hips around, and suddenly I see more than just his shiny red lips. Julian, with his long dark hair pulled up into a messy ponytail, grooving to a beat only he can hear... *attracts me.* I actually pop a woody. A sheen of moisture forms on my upper lip.

"Why were you sitting alone at lunch the other day?" I have no idea why I ask him this. The question just pops out of my mouth.

Julian stops dancing. His smile falls right off his face, and he looks at me directly. "Don't you know about me?"

After an awkward silence, Kandy and Anna both start talking at once, but Kandy speaks louder so we end up listening to her. "Last semester was kind of rocky for Julian. He felt very alone then... and sometimes he still feels that way now because of all the bleep he has to take from the other kids." As she gazes at Julian, her eyes fill up.

Her reply was sweet and the tears are touching, but they don't really explain anything.

Anna gets up, steps so she's standing right in front of Julian, and looks at him sort of like a mother would. "But now Julian has friends and this alliance, and even if he sits alone at lunch because Kandy and I have studio art that period, he knows that it's just lunch."

"Plus, he's allowed to eat in the office if he wants to," Kandy informs me, but she's still looking at him.

The atmosphere has changed in our little group; it's now charged with electricity. However, *I'm* not plugged into the current. There's something major I'm missing here, and *this* I'm sure of.

"I'll go next—I'll tell you guys about when I felt most excluded." Julian returns to his desk, and so Anna sits down too.

"You don't have to say anything you don't want to say, Julian," she reminds him.

Julian looks at her and smiles, but not with happiness. "I've felt excluded in school since I was in kindergarten—starting at circle time on the first day of school, to be precise—when Jamison Reeves called me a sissy. I've pretty much always felt like an outsider at school."

We all nod.

"But I felt excluded everywhere, really. Everywhere." Julian reaches up, pulls the elastic out of his hair, and what looks like a sheet of brown silk falls all over his shoulders. Some of it covers his face. "Anna and Kandy know this—I seriously thought everybody in this school did—but last fall, I tried to…."

His voice trails off, but I'm sure I know what he was going to say. And I want to stop him from spelling out the details of how he was feeling desperate enough to attempt suicide, but I can't. I just sit there and watch his pretty lips move, and I listen, as his words rip me apart.

"I confused a Ziploc baggie of Extra Strength Tylenol for a bag of Skittles, and, you know, I ate the whole damned thing." His eyes are hidden behind his dark hair and I'm glad. "Don't ask me why I did it, 'cause I won't tell you, Kale. But Anna and Kandy know. Anyway, when I felt most excluded was the day I returned to school after being out for almost two months." He stops talking for a few seconds, during which time I realize I'm drooling. I was listening to Julian so intently I actually forgot to swallow. "It was the stuff kids said to me that day— like they thought I *failed* because I didn't die."

The three of us stare at Julian, whose eyes we still can't see. And we're silent until Ms. Valencia approaches our group—Julian hiding behind his hairy veil, Anna and Kandy sniffling, and then there's shell-shocked me, eyes as round as Oreo cookies. "So have you discussed times you felt very *included* in school yet?"

"I feel included right now," Anna says.

"Me too," Kandy adds.

I already bared my soul once and am not willing to go there again.

"Very good. I think it's time to come together as a full group." She steps to the front of the room.

43

The girls' eyes are still fixed on Julian.

"I think you're brave for being so honest, Julian," says Anna.

"I know it was hard for you. I think you're brave too," Kandy agrees.

I think so too. But I don't say a word because I'm nowhere near as courageous.

Kale, 7:00 p.m.

HUGHIE IS acting strange. I think it's because he has to go to lunch with his mother on Saturday. He needs to chill out—it isn't such a big deal. But lately, the kid sleeps all the time, with the shades pulled down and the lights out, and it's a pain in the ass because this is *my* bedroom.

"I'm not going to stay out of my own bedroom because you need alone time to wallow in depression, Hughie." I lean over on the bed, and I snap my bedside light on.

"Nobody told you to keep the light off. I'll just pull my covers over my head."

"What's the big deal with one stupid lunch with Serenity, huh?" I slide my computer on my lap and check Facebook. "It'll be a done deal in one hour."

"You don't know Mary Pat like I know her, Kale. She's always got a plan."

He hasn't pulled the covers over his head yet, so I keep on talking. "What's she gonna do? Kidnap you?"

"Jeez—I hadn't thought of that...."

I search for Julian Mendez's Facebook page. We share a bunch of friends, kids from school who won't sit with him at lunch. "Weird."

"Not really. Mary Pat doesn't think straight all the time."

"I was talking about something else."

Hughie pulls his covers over his head. I guess our little chat is over, which is okay because I'm more interested in Julian's Facebook page. That girl Sydney Harper who makes fun of Hughie posted something nasty. And a lot of the student body of Crestdale High liked it.

44

I'm starting to get a picture of why Julian tried to end it all last fall. I'm not sure I could handle what he's dealing with here.

I wish I had courage to do what a REHO and GSA member should do.

But I don't.

Julian, 7:00 p.m.

FACEBOOK

Sydney Harper> Julian Mendez
Aren't you past your sell-by date? LOL.
57 likes 22 comments 10 shares

Sydney never misses an opportunity to remind me I'm late for my appointment to kiss the world goodbye. She's clever, though, and comes up with ways to send her message cryptically enough to avoid getting in trouble. The ability to persecute with subtlety is a true talent, and Sydney Harper has mastered it.

Nonetheless, my face gets red and I start sweating. And my heart beats faster than it did when I finally reached the top of the rope in gym class, thanks to Mr. Durante, the PE teacher, who offered to hold the knot at the bottom when no one else would.

I immediately deactivate my Facebook account. It isn't hard to do.

I'm tempted to delete it completely because right now I feel like I'm never going to want to go on social media again, especially not after I transition. But I've learned a thing or two since my unsuccessful attempt to bite the big one last fall. *Kudos to Dr. Evelyn.* One of these valuable lessons was to be less impulsive. I know I need to slow down and think this situation through, which I can't do when I'm hyperventilating. So instead of wiping myself off the face of the Facebook world, I relieve my pain by deactivating the Julian Mendez account so that I'm only semigone, and then I concentrate on slowing my breathing.

Facebook deactivation is a temporary situation. I can choose to make it permanent down the road, if I want. Just like I can choose to finish high school with the state's free online program. Mama and I have already had several virtual meetings with the guidance counselors.

Comforting thoughts.

CHAPTER 6—THURSDAY

Julian, 3:00 a.m.

IT HAPPENED again.

I lie in bed, shivering so violently that my teeth actually chatter. Then I pull the sheet up to my shoulders, over my chest, which is dripping with cold sweat. It doesn't help. I'm cold and hot—my body has no clue which temperature is going to win this battle.

I still have soul-sucking nightmares about the day I tried to die—dreams about the loneliness, the anxiety, and the hopelessness that brought me to the point that I thought it would be better to be gone. It all started as a flicker of an idea about how much easier everything would be... if I didn't have to *be* anymore. Soon, though, that tiny spark of contemplation wormed its way into my consciousness. And even though I pushed it away, the pesky thing kept coming back. The brilliant and freaking terrifying idea I had for ending my pain came back and came back until it became a real option. Until it became the best option.

I'd been rejected by everybody at school a long time ago. *That was old news.* My isolation there *almost* didn't bother me anymore. I told myself over and over again that alone was how I liked it—how I *wanted* it. Part of me even believed this.

As of last fall, only a few kids still wasted their energy on bullying me, unless you consider acting with total indifference toward somebody a manner of putting them down. To most kids, I was too insignificant to bully. I was nothing, except to Sydney Harper, and thus to her devoted followers. Sydney knew I was an academic threat—and she used every means possible to push me over the edge that I was already teetering on.

But to be real, what I tried to do to myself that day wasn't because of my loneliness, though it didn't help. I did what I did because of my body. Because of what was happening to my body in terms of a word I'd grown to hate: *puberty.*

I still detest the *sound* of that word.

But I *was not* the person I was turning into. My child's body was far preferable to the hairy, deep-voiced beast with constant hard-ons who was taking me over.

I put all logic aside—the certainty of my mother's future suffering included—and headed into what I saw as the light at the end of a short and torturous tunnel that had been my life. That day, when I climbed up the rickety ladder into the ancient tree house in the only tree in the apartment building's yard, I was more truly trying to climb out of a pit of despair. I saw relief in what I was going to do up there.

It sounds dramatic, but making the decision to kill yourself isn't exactly humdrum. Back then it seemed like my only option, because I couldn't figure out how to live in a body that wasn't mine.

And so, once again, I wake up sweating, because in my sleep I was leaning on the splintering wall of that stupid tree house, sucking away at a bottle of tropical Gatorade, scared to toss the next handful of pills in my mouth, but more scared not to. And having no words to explain to my mother how what was happening to my body was screwing with my mind. Like every single time I wake from this very same dream, I'm assailed by an image of Mama in the hospital, wearing on *her* face the pain that for so long lived in *my* heart—and knowing I put it there.

"Ma!" I'm such a damned coward. I was a coward on the day I tried to take my own life and leave my mother with nothing but five words scribbled on the back of a gum wrapper, and I'm a coward now.

But maybe it's okay to be a coward, if you admit you're one. "Mama!"

I'm faster on my feet than she is, so instead of waiting for my mother to come to me, I jump out of my bed and run down the short hall, throw open her bedroom door where she's already sitting up, about to push herself from the bed. "Jules! Are you okay?"

Her arms come around me, and I'm safe in a way I didn't know I could be safe last October. "I dreamed about it again…."

Mama pulls me down so I'm lying on her chest. I know I'm not too heavy because my body is still mostly a kid's, thanks to the puberty blockers. "You did the right thing by coming to me, Jules. You've always got me to turn to. You hear me?"

"Uh-huh." I want to cry but tears don't come. I think I cried them all last fall and there are none left. "I hate waking you up—you've gotta work in the morning."

Mama's grip tightens on my shoulders. "I woke up for you when you were a hungry baby and a piss-wet boy, and dammit, I'll wake up for you now." Her voice is firm.

"Can I stay?"

"You think I'd let you outta my sight?" *I love her so much.*

"I'm such a pain in the ass." We both laugh.

"A pain my ass couldn't live without. Now lie down beside me and tell your mama about what happened at school today."

Incidentally, the note said, *I can't take it anymore*. But I never knew I could turn to my mother, and she would change things this way.

CHAPTER 7—FRIDAY

Kale, 8:00 p.m.

WHERE IS he... where is he... where is he.... Where. Is. He?

At lunch on Monday, two days before he told me he tried to kill himself by downing a bag of pain medicine, Julian told me, "So I guess I'll see you Friday night." Not that the news impacted me in such a way that made it hard for me to fall asleep for the past several nights, because I couldn't stop picturing Julian semiconscious in his tree house. *It didn't.* I've been having trouble falling asleep because I'm struggling in Spanish III, that's all.

So why do I care that he's not here?

"We gather tonight in the spirit of love and selflessness, and with the solemn hope that our efforts to serve the community will be sufficient to keep hope alive for those who struggle to obtain the rights inherent to all human beings."

Tonight, instead of doing the standard hand-holding thing, we've crossed our arms in front of ourselves, per Judy's instructions, and are grasping each other's hands this way.

Welcome to *Variations in Hand-holding 101.*

"I thought it might be fun," Judy says, unsuccessfully fighting her urge to giggle, "if we started our meeting tonight by passing a hand squeeze around the circle, as we bond over our common concern— ridding the world of all forms of discrimination." She peeks around the circle with a sheepish look on her face. "It might be fun... I think... so I'll start."

I look up and sharply to the left in an effort to catch eyes with the very tall girl who is again holding my hand. When she glances down at me and I send her a look that clearly asks, "Are we at a human rights organization meeting or in preschool?" But she quickly shrugs and looks away, totally sold on this faux bonding technique. I'm left to wait for the squeeze to come my way so I can pass it on and become one with these relative strangers. Before the squeeze makes its way all the way around the circle, though, our meeting is interrupted.

"I'm late. So sue me." Julian stops at the bottom of the stairs and strikes a dramatic pose—his right hip jutting out to the side while he scrutinizes his fingernails.

I try to ignore my relief when I see him, but that would be like trying to ignore a tropical cyclone blowing past the tiki hut I'm trying to sleep in on the beach. In other words, it doesn't work.

"Oh, Julian, hello, and welcome back to REHO. We're so happy you could make it tonight. Please, join the circle. You're going to need to cross your arms, though." Judy warns, and her face is beet red. "We're passing around a hand squeeze in the name of bonding. It's a little bit tricky with your arms crossed." She waits while Julian steps into the circle between tall girl and me. "I'll start over again. How does that sound?"

When Julian glances up at me, I see "What the hell is this?" in his eyes, and I decide Judy has succeeded in her goal, if not in exactly the manner she'd intended. Julian and I have bonded over what we both consider to be a juvenile activity. Or better yet, a stupid exercise in attempting to force emotional connection between relative strangers.

I receive a sharp squeeze to my right hand and immediately and obediently send it off to Julian.

"Flirt." He says it so quietly I'm not quite sure he actually said it. Maybe I just wish he said it. And he doesn't look up at me again until it's time for us to scatter the throw pillows on the floor. "Get me the purple one," he says with a nod.

"Huh?" Did Julian just demand I fetch him a pillow? And after suggesting I was flirting with him. *Was* I flirting with him?

"The purple pillow. I want *that* one." I look down into dark eyes that are sparkling persuasively. Or is it… is that *glitter* shimmering on his eyelids?

Side note: Glitter used to be made of glass and metal but now it's mainly made of plastic. It's a decoration that reflects light, causing it to look like it is actually sparkling.

How on earth do I even know this?

"Wait here and I'll get it for you." I turn and rush toward the closet with the rest of the commoners, shaking my head at my eagerness to please this guy.

From behind me I hear Julian's voice. "I knew you'd see it my way."

Soon we're all seated on our pillows waiting for what comes next. Judy, from her pillow in the front of the room, clears her throat. "I thought that tonight we might focus on one of the important issues personally challenging a member of our group." We all look around at each other as if *please help me* will be stamped in bold black print on the forehead of the needy member. "As many of you know, Edna's dear husband Wilbur passed away last spring." Again, we all look around the room and notice that Edna isn't here.

"And she has struggled with issues related to age discrimination."

"W-w-where is she to-to-tonight?" asks Tom, the man who never stutters when he sings. "I t-t-talked to her l-last night and she said she was gonna b-b-be c-c-c-oming."

"Well, the sad fact is, Edna took a fall this morning while crossing the street in front of the Beautiful Sunset Senior Center, where she lives," Judy informs us. "She told me on the phone that the traffic light there does not leave her enough time to cross, so she was rushing and stumbled… and ended up falling flat on her face. Broke a tooth, she did."

"Oh no."

"Poor Edna."

"I hope it wasn't a front tooth."

I twirl a stubby dreadlock, irrationally angry. "That's just not right," I say to nobody.

Billy rises from his pillow, which is actually a stained, child-sized beanbag chair. "Age discrimination is as inhumane as racism. We need to do something about this! Let me tell you…."

"REHO must unite!" Tall girl thrusts her fist into the air, completely enraged. I hadn't even imagined that she possessed a fierce side until now.

"We also need to do whatever is necessary to help Edna through her crisis," points out Karima, the young Muslim woman. "We must show our respect by carrying her burden."

Judy looks like the Cheshire Cat, grinning smugly on a ratty old couch cushion. "This is exactly the response I was hoping for. Let's break into groups and come up with ideas about how we can repair our society with regard to this example of age discrimination... shall we?"

I end up in the Crosswalk Timers Group with the tall girl, whose name is Paulina, Tom, and Julian. We plan our task, which is to go to the actual crosswalk in front of the Beautiful Sunset Senior Center on Bay Road and investigate whether there's sufficient time for an elderly person, a disabled person, and a parent with a child in a stroller to safely cross the wide street.

"My mother works at the senior center so I know the lay of the land really well. Let's make a video," Julian proposes. "We can reveal the truth."

It's a brilliant idea.

To be real, in my life so far, I haven't been inspired to do much that makes a difference in the world. And I'm talking about the passionate kind of inspired, not just the "Yeah, sure, I could get into doing that" kind of inspired. I'm a decent student—not great—and I enjoy collecting random facts about arbitrary topics. I've become an insect-relocator and I feel bad when I think about the slaughtering of innocent animals to fill my plate at dinnertime, so I don't eat meat. I wear hemp and organic cotton clothes, mostly because it's politically correct for a blossoming hippie. But I haven't stepped up and made a difference, and when Julian says, "Let's make a video"—a video of people walking across a street— I'm more motivated than I think I've ever been before.

"I'll b-b-bring my grandma Tilly. We can see if sh-she-she can get across the street before the l-l-light changes."

"Great, Tom... that's your name, right?"

"Th-that's right, I'm T-t-tom." Tom looks at Julian like he's our leader.

"I know a guy who got hit by an SUV last year. He has all kinds of steel rods implanted in his right leg to hold it together, and he walks with a limp. I can see if he's busy—like maybe on Sunday afternoon. Would that work?" Paulina speaks directly to Julian too.

He nods and replies, "Sunday works for me. How about you guys?" Tom and I nod.

"Great. Let's meet in front of the elderly housing building at say, noon on Sunday. And don't be late. My ball gown turns back into rags at three o'clock." Julian is stepping up to the plate as the official head of the Crosswalk Timers Group. He's a natural leader in this setting and it's cool. I feel a strange pull in my heart.

Hmmm... is it possible that Julian Mendez is tugging on my heartstrings? Is that even a thing?

My face gets hot and I'm glad nobody can read my mind. For the next forty-five minutes, we go over the details of our plans for Sunday afternoon, and before I'm ready, the meeting is ending. Without being asked, I pick up my pillow and Julian's purple pillow and return them to the closet, as it just seems like the right thing to do. But when I turn around to say goodbye, Julian's already gone. I'm irrationally disappointed, which is closely followed by my standard "why do I care?" attitude. I grab my locally raised eco-organic wool peacoat from the rack in the corner, say a few quick goodbyes, and head upstairs to the street.

It's started to drizzle outside, which is going to melt the snow and turn the streets into sheets of ice by tomorrow morning. Too bad it'll be a Saturday morning—if it were a school day there would be a delay. *What a waste!*

I jog down the sidewalk toward the parking lot behind the pharmacy with my coat over my head; I live in fear of the wet-dog-dreads smell. Mom's minivan is cold, but at least it's dry inside. I start the engine and crank up the heat. As I pull out of the parking lot, I see a slim figure standing at the bus stop, rain pouring down on his man bun, his thin black trench coat drenched.

Without hesitation, I pull my car right up beside him and lower the passenger window. "Hop in, dude. I'll give you a lift home."

The strangest thing happens. Julian steps back, away from the minivan, and looks down at the wet pavement. "No. No, I'm fine."

"You aren't fine. You're soaking wet. So get in."

When Julian looks at me, it isn't with that get-a-life expression I've come to expect. Instead, Julian looks scared. "I said no. No, thank you."

I want to argue with him. I want to tell him he's being stupid and his pretty hair is getting all wet, *so get in the damned van.* Just like I'd do if he were Hughie. But this other part of me wants to whine, *"Why-y-y won't you get in?"* and then inform him that nobody's scared of me... *nobody.* I'm never the one to hurt people first. I only counterpunch when attacked! I wouldn't even step on a bug—literally.

I do neither of these things.

"Have it your way," I say tersely and drive off.

CHAPTER 8—SATURDAY

Kale, noon

I DON'T know why Dad thinks it's *my* job to chaperone Hughie on this ridiculous farce of a lunch date with his topless go-go dancer mother. *Jeez,* I'm too busy to be anybody's babysitter. I have Grateful Dead music to download and garbage to compost.

"Can't believe Uncle Sam is forcing me to meet up with my mother," Hughie complains as I pull the minivan into a parking spot.

"Making *us* meet her," I correct him.

"Uh, yeah… sorry about that, Crunchy." We get out of the minivan and head for the restaurant.

"If you're *so sorry*, dude, then tell me to take a hike. I'll come back and pick you up at one. Not a problem for me." I don't even try to hide the sarcasm in my voice as I make this suggestion.

Hughie gasps, and for a second I think he's choking on his chewing gum. Then he barks, "No! You're coming with me or I'm not doing it!" I don't get why he's so freaked out. After all, it's just his mother.

We get out of the van and head for the Sinking Stone Mall's food pavilion where the Shopper's Retreat Café is slowly filling with mostly girls clutching plastic bags filled with their finds at the Saturday Morning Biweekly Sale Event. Mom has been here for hours already, as Dad dropped her off at precisely 9:30 a.m. when the doors opened. She tells us time and again that all the good deals are gone by noon. Lucky that Mom rents a storage unit downtown, or we wouldn't have room in the house for all the "good deals."

"We have to pick up my mother at one fifteen outside of the Shoe Depot so I can get her to her pedicure appointment across town by one thirty. We have seventy minutes to get this lunch thing done, not a minute more."

Hughie looks at me sideways and mumbles something about lunch with Mary Pat being seventy minutes too long.

The abject horror I see in his eyes leads me to conclude that the kid is under some serious, if inexplicable, stress. It won't kill me to stop being a complete asshole.

"Look Hughie, I know this isn't exactly what either of us wants to be doing with a Saturday, but... but the sweet potato fries here don't suck at all and... and you like vanilla frappes... and I'm buying." Well, Dad is forking out the dough for lunch, but it's basically the same thing.

Hughie just shrugs, as usual not too talkative, but at least he doesn't look like he's about to projectile vomit anymore. We head across the parking lot.

Aunt Serenity is waiting for us in the lobby of the Shopper's Retreat Café. She rushes over and hugs Hughie rather aggressively. His body goes limp as a rag doll, and he doesn't hug her back.

"Hi, Kalin! Hey, my little Hughie-bear! Hope you're hungry for lunch." Serenity looks like she just stepped off the beach. Her leathery skin is perfectly tanned and her long waves of shiny blonde hair are stiffly windswept off her face. She's wearing what looks like one of those fringy, white, shift-thingies that ladies wear to cover up their bathing suits. With thigh-high spike-heeled boots. *Jeez—it's January.*

"Nice to see you, Aunt Serenity." I glare at my wet noodle of a cousin who is casually slithering out from beneath his mother's purple pointy-nailed grasp.

"Well, don't you have something to say to your momsie?" Serenity latches on to Hughie's shoulder again, tighter than before, and gawks at her son with wide baby blue eyes.

Once again, Hughie looks super close to barfing, but he grunts, "Nice claws, Mary Pat."

I shudder at Hughie's rudeness, but Aunt Serenity howls with laughter. "*You likey, baby boy?* Got 'em done over at the Inspired Fingernail Crafters in Jamestown. See the tiny panthers stenciled on my thumbnails?" She releases Hughie just long enough to display her thumbs, side by side. Then she growls and claws the air. "And you know

57

I don't like it when you call me Mary Pat. It's Momsie." She reattaches herself to his lifeless arm and adds, "Or Serenity."

Hughie sighs too deliberately for my comfort, and I decide it's past time to find a table. Since it's a seat-yourself restaurant, I lead our group to a table in the most distant corner, farthest from the windows that overlook the mall. All I need is to be seen by kids from school breaking bread with my socially challenged cousin and his mother, a middle-aged go-go dancer from the town's only strip joint.

Tough to talk my way out of that one.

And there it is again—haunting memories of Judy and REHO—and of course, Julian—and the fact that my cause in life is human rights activism. It shouldn't matter to me how much Serenity resembles a weathered Dolly Parton in skimpy beach attire, or which body parts she has to wiggle to pay the bills. But... yes, there's a big but here and it isn't Serenity's backside I'm referring to—her butt is small and tight from all of the dancing. It's just that Aunt Serenity is so self-centered. Not that I expect her to be a pole-dancing Mother Theresa, but she could actually listen to what her kid says every once in a while.

As soon as we're seated, Aunt Serenity starts in on Hughie. "So, baby, I saw your name in the newspaper the other day." She stops talking, bats her thick, black eyelashes, and clears her throat.

"You read the newspaper?" Hughie asks, surprised.

"Ah, who am I trying to kid? The only thing I read is the channel guide on DIRECTV." A long sniff and a snorting sound follow her confession. "One of the guys at the lounge told me he read that you won some sort of science fair. Your momsie would've liked to have seen your project."

"You wouldn't have gotten what it was about." Hughie stares at the placemat on the table in front of him. I don't think he has looked his mother in the eye yet. Not that he ever looks anybody in the eye. But today he's different than usual, more distant than I've ever seen him before. I wonder if being forced to see his mother today might be some kind of a last straw on his back.

"Try me, son. Your momsie is smarter than she looks. Hell, you got your brains from somewhere, and it sure wasn't from Big Al at the town garage, who I strongly suspect is your daddy."

"My sperm donor," Hughie mumbles, and I will admit to feeling bad for him.

"So, you got yourself a girlfriend yet?" Aunt Serenity is now resting her ginormous breasts on the table, one on either side of her bread plate. In her defense, they're too heavy to hold up without help.

"I *study*, Mary Pat. I'm not looking for friends or girlfriends— I'm just looking for a college scholarship that gets me the hell out of Crestdale."

"Well, that attitude certainly isn't going to get you a girlfriend."

Thankfully, the waiter comes and rattles off a list of today's specials, none of which is vegetarian, but his little food speech serves as a necessary distraction.

After we order, Aunt Serenity's inquisition of her son continues. "Listen, sugar bear, I was thinking… there's no reason you can't come back and live with me. I have a one-bedroom apartment now, and a nice pullout couch that could be all yours. And I'm closer to the school than you are at Sam's house. It'd only take you twenty minutes to walk, and if you stuck your thumb out, you could get to school in five. Wouldn't that be nice? Wouldn't it, sugar bear?"

Talk about detached. Hughie is staring at Aunt Serenity's five-inch heel, purple-suede thigh boots, and instead of appearing righteously scandalized, he looks just plain distraught. His wild green eyes scream, *Save me, Kale!*

So I step in to pull Hughie's backside out of the fire. "It's like this, Aunt Serenity—Hughie's all set up at our house. You know, he's got his books and his computer and his clothes, and it would be hard for him to move—" My argument is shabby at best, which is why it's so easy for my aunt to cut off midsentence.

"All of those things will fit nicely on the shelf in my living room and in the skinny hall closet, once I clean out last year's cowgirl costumes… I've got a half-dozen pairs of assless chaps that have seen better days, you know?" She sends me a "shut up or I will make you suffer" glare and then refocuses on Hughie. "Baby, I miss having you with me. I swear that I won't bring so many of my *gentlemen friends* back to the room after work. And when I do, we'll keep the door shut and the volume down, and I mean it this time."

Hughie's jaw drops in the way I'm accustomed to, but this time I don't reach over and shut it with the side of my hand. I can't. I'm in shock too.

"I'm gonna talk to Sam about when we can move you home. I still haven't scraped up enough cash to buy a car, so we're gonna need to use your aunt Kathy's minivan to move you back in, but that's no biggie." Aunt Serenity isn't aware that her son is freaking out. "Like, I'm thinking maybe we can do it next Sunday, but it can't be 'til after I throw this naughty nighty party I promised Amy Jo I'd have. She just isn't making ends meet, now that she's only dancing afternoon shifts. FYI, it's true that businessmen don't tip as good as truckers."

We both stare at her. My mouth is now hanging open too, as what she's saying is an uncomfortable combination of TMI and *what the hell?* And something about Hughie is different. He's not just distant—he has completely checked out of this lunch date.

"What are you guys looking at me like *that* for?" Aunt Serenity is defensive. "The tips aren't as good in the afternoon as at night. And tips are the lifeblood of the professional dancer." Once again, she's missed the point.

I do this shrug-nod thing—I'm not sure what Hughie does—but I'm relieved he doesn't say what we're both thinking: *Serenity, you're a stripper. You did not attend the Juilliard School to study modern dance.*

We're served lunch, which my brosin and I stuff down rather hastily. Both of us just want this lunch date to come to a premature conclusion.

"God, you two must be starving! Isn't Aunty Kathy feeding you boys?" Aunt Serenity asks. "No worries, Kalin, you can come over to dinner at our place any time you want. My specialty is heating up those frozen chicken pot pies—the ones with dark meat and peas and those little pearly onions."

Hughie doesn't even look up when he says, "Kale's an herbivore. Remember?"

She tilts her head and asks, "Kalin smokes weed?"

"Mary Pat, Kale's a *vegetarian*. He won't eat chicken pot pie."

Aunt Serenity turns to me. "So you think you're too good for my chicken pot pie? I have a feeling Mrs. Stouffer would have something to say about that."

This conversation is going nowhere. And fast. "We need to head out soon. I have to pick up my mother at the Shoe Depot in a few minutes."

"I have to run too. Got me a double shift of bootie shaking coming up. Two in the afternoon till two in the morning." Aunt Serenity places one pointy thumbnail between her teeth and bites down on the tiny panther stenciled there. "I figure I'll roll my hips two thousand times in twelve hours, at fifty cents per rotation, which adds up to—*cha-ching*—the big bucks. How's that for mathematics, Hughie-bear?" Again, she claws the air, purring with satisfaction.

Hughie groans softly and then goes to that place in his head where he seems to find shelter.

"Well, thanks for meeting us, Aunt Mary—I mean, Aunt Serenity. I'm gonna head over to the cashier now to pay for lunch." I glance at Hughie, who has momentarily returned from the land of the lost. There's an unhealthy dose of panic in his eyes at the prospect of being alone with his own flesh and blood. "It'll only take two minutes," I say to calm him down, but it doesn't work.

"I gotta take a leak, so I'll catch ya later, Mary Pat." He's off of his chair and on his way to the men's room before I can blink.

Looks like I have to step up to the plate. Again. I lean over the table and give Aunt Serenity a hug, trying to avoid brushing her boobs with my wrists, which is challenging. "It was nice to see you." The standard goodbye—my father raised me right while my mother was at the mall.

"Thanks for paying for lunch, Kalin. And I'll leave the tip. I have too many singles bills to count!" She squeezes my arms and winks at me. "Occupational hazard."

Julian, 7:00 p.m.

As SOON as I get into my bedroom, I pull off every stitch of socially acceptable boy's clothes and throw on the pink silky nighty that I stuck under my pillow when I forced myself to stop being Julia this morning. It doesn't happen automatically—putting the boy back on in the morning after being myself all night. Maybe it sounds kind of strange, but every day when I wake up and take off my nightgown, I stand naked beside my bed for maybe five minutes, because that's how long it takes me to numb my body and spirit. When I've managed to make my mind go blank, I pull together all the scrappy remnants of my boy-self, so I can stick on my androgynous uniform and face life as a guy.

Then at night I have to work just as hard at letting the stress of being someone I'm not drain out of my body. I lie down on my bed and stare up at the stained powder blue ceiling, and then I cross and uncross my legs, over and over, relishing the smoothness because it reminds me of who I really am. Next, I collect all the stress in my belly and push it down to my feet so it can drip out of my toes. This is usually hard to do, but tonight it pours out of me without too much effort.

It's been a long day, and knowing Mama has to work tomorrow morning, after not having even one weekend day to rest, kills me. I hate that she has to run herself ragged to make the payments on my GnRH treatments.

Mama says seeing me happy again, now that my body is stalled in its early stage of puberty, makes it more than worth her effort. I know that she means it and that she's happy because I can see it in her eyes when she looks at me. But it's all mixed in with her fear that I might try to hurt myself again.

The heavy burden of guilt forces the air out of my chest.

On the way home from Norwell today, Mama told me that Dr. Isabel's staff from the Children's Gender Center knows what to do when an insurance company, like ours, "excludes care for transgender services." Yeah, it's a PC way of saying, "We ain't gonna pay for that freaky shit!" The office manager is going to send our insurance company a set of guidelines for the endocrine treatment of transgender people. And with the guide, Dr. Isabel will attach a letter that insists my puberty blockers and future Hormone Replacement Therapy are a medical necessity and that they should be covered. She convinced Mama that it was worth at least *trying* to get them to provide services for me. *For us.*

The thought of *us*—Mama and me—makes me smile. We're like a very small, very strong team.

I could tell she was hopeful, and I'll admit to getting that "OMG, maybe this can save us" feeling too. But I've always been a realistic person, and so now that I have time to lie here and think it over, I doubt that any big company is gonna shell out cash they could keep. But I *know* I'm a girl, even if my body tells the world a different story… and even though I've tried for so many years to be a boy.

I'm a girl, a real girl. I know this to be true. *Nothing* can stop this from being true.

My phone dings with a text message. I'm so deep in thought, the little ding makes me jump a mile.

Kandy: *Julian—your Facebook! It's gone! You ok?*

Julian: *I'm fine. Take a chill pill, girl.*

Kandy: *I'll take a chill pill AFTER you tell me where your FB page went.*

Julian: *Believe me, you don't wanna know.*

Kandy: *I'LL tell you what I wanna know. So spill.*

Julian: *It's not worth my time or yours, but if you have to know, I temporarily deactivated FB to sidestep incoming bullshit.*

Kandy: *The Sydney Harper variety of flying BS?*

Julian: *I can't get a thing past you.*

Kandy: *I'm sorry you have to deal with that. I'll tell you what—I'll go to guidance on Monday and report her for cyber bullying. And more—because she physically bullied you in the hall the other morning.*

Julian: *Please don't. That was no big deal and neither is this. Like I said, I'm fine. But it's looking more and more like I'm gonna have to get schooled online when I move forward with the whole "Julia" thing.*

Kandy: *There are ways around it, Julian. You have Anna and me to support you after your transition and there are plenty of teachers, like Ms. Valencia, for example, who will knock themselves out trying to support you. You won't be alone. So please don't rush into a decision.*

Julian: *Now, do I seem like the kind of girl to do that?*

Kandy: *LOL, um, yes.*

Julian: *Well, thanks for checking in on me. Long day in the city. Gonna hit the hay, K?*

Kandy: *OK. Love ya, Julian.*

Julian: *Not as much as I love you.*

And I mean it, but Kandy doesn't have to know just how true it is.

Chapter 9—Sunday

Julian, 11:00 a.m.

"MAMA, I'M going out!" I yell as I put the finishing touches on my eyeliner. *Cat eyes rock.*

"It's my day off and I'm planted on the couch—you need to think again if you expect my ass to move!" she bellows in reply. "Come down here if you want to talk to me, Jules!"

I trot down the stairs and swing around the corner into the living room where Mama's eyes are glued to the widescreen. "*What Not to Wear*, Ma? *Really?* You don't need that show—let *me* take you shopping and we'll get your wardrobe all straightened out."

"Maybe I don't trust you, Jules. You'll have me dressed like a pissed-off teenager." She eyes my Goth outfit pointedly.

"I think I might be insulted. Do you really doubt that I know how to create a tasteful and classy ensemble?"

"Nah, how could I doubt you after that gourmet omelet you made for me this morning? Now, come here and give Mama a kiss and a hug, and tell me where you're heading off to."

Ever since my failed attempt to meet my maker last fall, my mother has shown an obsessive interest in how I spend my free time. "Just out, that's all."

Mama grunts and shifts her feet down to the floor, and then she tugs her pajama pants, I'm assuming, out of the crack of her ass. "Not good enough. Are you meeting up with Anna and Kandy?"

I reach in my pocket and pull out my tube of lip gloss. "Try again," I tell her before rolling on the shine.

My mother looks like she could use an afternoon at the spa. Her long dark hair is frizzy and graying noticeably around the temples, and her round face is more furiously pink than usual. And I hate it

65

when her eyes look tired. "This isn't twenty questions, Julian, and I've got no clue."

"It's like this, Mama. I joined a town club."

Mama struggles to lift herself off the couch. "I don't believe it. When you were eleven, you quit the Little Buttercup Girls after I went to bat to get you into that group. You aren't the town club type, Jules."

"There's no need to get up, Mama.... It's a human rights *organization*. Dr. Evelyn thinks it'd be good for me."

She eases herself back down and grunts, "Smart gal, that Dr. Evelyn. And I always said so, for the record."

"Today we're getting together to prove that the crosswalk in front of the Beautiful Sunset Senior Center doesn't allow certain people enough time to cross the road."

"Certain people? People like me! I move a little slower than most because of my size, and every day before work I have to jog to get across that road in the time the crosswalk allows me."

The fact that it'll be helping Mama makes this job ten times more important to me. "Well, no worries, Ma, because I'm on it. And I left a brownie for you on the kitchen counter. It's wrapped in a paper towel."

"You're too sweet, baby."

I know a few people who would disagree with that sentiment. I grab the plate of brownies I made for Edna from the kitchen and then head for the bus stop.

Kale, 12:15 p.m.

WITH JULIAN'S help, Edna hobbles along the walkway to the cluster of benches where the Crosswalk Timers Group sits awaiting its unofficial leader. I'm glad he's focused on Edna and not on me, because I don't know how to feel about him right now. On Friday night after REHO, *he* refused *my* offer of a ride home, and let's face it—*I'm* the normal one in this potential friendship scenario.

"I am so very touched that you all have come here today to help out!" Like the first time I met her, I'm surprised by the sharp voice that comes out of such a frail-looking person. "And Julian, how did you know I was craving chocolate? I'll eat the brownies you made me with my cup of tea tonight before bed."

He actually baked Edna brownies?

Julian helps Edna to one of the sturdy wooden benches where she sits down.

"Edna, p-p-please m-m-meet m-my grandma, T-t-tilly Madison. W-we're gonna time her w-w-walking across the s-street."

The two elderly women lean across the bench to shake hands. "Thank you for coming, Tilly."

"Well, I'm very proud that my grandson wants to make a difference by working to improve the state of human rights." Tom's grandmother, Tilly, is old, but is still *sprightly* and *spry*—two SAT words. Now that I've used them, I own them. In theory.

Paulina steps forward and declares, "I brought along my friend Rodney today. He goes to Crestdale Community College with me." She rests her hand on his shoulder and closes her eyes for a second, as if she's trying to memorize how it feels to touch him. Weird. "He's the one I was telling you guys about, remember? The guy who got hit by a Jeep Cherokee...."

Rodney is a burly, unshaven guy with a ski hat pulled down to his ears. He's about a foot shorter than Paulina, but that doesn't seem to dull his shine in her eyes. She's super into him.

Julian steps forward and shakes his hand in that same ladylike way he shook mine when I met him. "Sorry to hear about the Jeep attack, Rodney. That must've been a damned bad day. And thanks for coming to help."

"Not a problem, man." Rodney sounds as gritty as he looks.

Within a few minutes, the Crosswalk Timers Group is doing what we were created to do. Tilly is winded, having crossed the wide street four times, as Paulina timed her with the stopwatch on her phone. On two of her four tries, Tilly didn't have enough time to get all the way across the street, and my job was to hold back traffic so that she could reach the sidewalk in one piece. Now that she's finished, I help her up the stairs so she can sit on the bench beside Edna and watch as Rodney begins his adventures in street crossing.

Julian is standing on the next bench to the right beside Edna and Tilly, making a video of all the crossing attempts on his phone. "When I get home, I'll download all this onto my computer and make a video that we can bring to the city transportation department," he tells me.

I get one of those heart-pulling feelings again, and say, "Good thinking, dude." It's lame, but at least I said something. Now I stand here gawking at him. Today he's wearing something I don't think I've ever seen on a guy except maybe on Aladdin in the Disney movie. Julian is wearing silky gray... genie pants. Yeah, genie pants. And they look really good. I mean, not hippie-good, and *I* wouldn't be caught dead in them, but they work for Julian, with his dark skin and long hair and the silver scarf tossed around his neck—it's all very magic-carpet-riding cool.

"So, you gotta get the crossing times from Paulina, for Tilly and Rodney, and I want you to average them for each person," Julian tells me.

I'm tempted to ask, "Who died and made you prince?" But I don't. I just nod because I'm kind of mesmerized by him. This is my very strange, but predictable, reaction to Julian.

It's just that his lips are shinier today than they were at REHO on Friday night.

I've never given too much thought to my sexuality, as I've been too busy obsessing over other things, like whether I best embody a hippie, an emo guy, or a prepster. Even so, I'm your everyday, average teenager when it comes to sexual urges. In other words, if I'm alone in my bedroom and the door is closed, it would be wise to knock before you barge in if you don't want to see something you'll have trouble forgetting. But since meeting Julian, I'm not sure exactly who to fantasize about when I'm alone in my room, getting busy with myself. A girl? A guy? Julian, himself?

And last night I found myself taking "The How Gay Am I? Quiz" online, in an effort to figure out what I'm supposed to be into, in terms of things more intimate than ways to keep the earth green.

Side note: In "The How Gay Am I? Quiz," I answered questions about my preferences regarding colors and cities and Lady Gaga songs and presidents. Favorite root vegetables and preferred rude hand gestures were also question topics. Confidentially, my result was that I am "Pretty Gay." I have not yet decided how I'm going to react to this.

I think he may be wearing lip gloss. I'd like to find out what it tastes like.

"Hey, Kale, look!" Julian jumps off the bench and points. "See that lady?"

He's so excited—I haven't seen him like this before. His eyes, though still as dark as ever, look bright, and I think it's because they're… sparkling. And not because he's wearing glitter eye shadow like that other time. "Dude?"

Julian grabs my wrist and drags me toward the stairs. "See that lady with the baby carriage and the little kid walking beside her?"

"Yeah, I see her."

"She's the conclusion of our video. Come on!"

We run down the stairs and along the sidewalk toward the lady with the two kids, Julian shouting for her to stop. I yell, "Dude, she's gonna call the cops on us!"

"Nah, she's gonna be a movie star!" he counters.

Julian runs off ahead of me, and when he catches up to the woman, he immediately starts negotiating. I can tell by the way he's talking with his hands and pantomiming a fall and pointing to his tooth that he's trying to get her to see things his way. She shakes her head, but he doesn't give up. He points to the baby and then to the little boy and starts waving his hands again. This time when he stops ranting, the lady shrugs and then nods, and just like that, Julian wins.

"I knew you'd see it my way," he says to her when I reach his side. "Kale, this nice lady just volunteered to let us time her as she crosses the road with her cute little kids in tow."

"Volunteered? *Hello?*" the young mother retorts. "On what planet do you call being badgered into saying yes *volunteering?*"

"And we are *so* appreciative, ma'am." Julian smiles and bats his eyelashes a few times. "Kale, why don't you lead the lady and her children to the crosswalk where we're conducting the experiment."

I'm freaking out. We've harassed a perfectly innocent young mother into doing our bidding. I fiddle with my dreadlocks but make no move to usher the mother to the crosswalk.

"Kale. Wake up and do your job. *REHO*, remember?" He's serious about what we're trying to accomplish.

The harshness in his voice breaks me out of my trance. Instead of verbally punching back, I murmur, "Oh… oh, yeah. We're doing the timing over there, by that crosswalk." The mother follows along behind me, pushing her baby carriage and maneuvering her little boy so he doesn't wander away.

Within fifteen minutes we have videotaped and timed the lady crossing the road four times with her now-cranky children. And she clearly did not have enough time—not even once out of her four reluctant attempts to get safely across the road in the time that was allotted by the lights.

After thanking the woman, the Crosswalk Timers Group reunites by the benches in front of the Beautiful Sunset Senior Center.

"I have all the footage I need to make a stellar video. And it will clearly show that the elderly, disabled, and people with small children cannot cross the street safely in the time allotted by the lights." Julian looks proud.

And I want to hug him, which is inexplicable.

Edna's also glowing. "And to have the crosswalk lights set up in such a way in front of an elderly housing center, well, it's just disgraceful. It is ageism at its boldest!"

"You said it, sister!" Tilly and Edna high-five. I rub my eyes because I'm not sure I just saw two eighty-year-old women slapping palms, but then they do it again with their other hands.

"Great work, everybody." Julian has risen to the level of the Crosswalk Timers Group's Grand Poobah. "I'll put this all together into a video we can show on Friday night at REHO. And if everybody approves, we can submit it to the city."

"I'll average all of the times of the street crossings and maybe I can get it to you at school this week," I say. My voice sounds so embarrassingly hopeful. "Like maybe at lunch tomorrow."

"Works for me," Julian says, grabbing his messenger bag from the bench. "Edna, do you need a hand getting back up to your room?"

"Why, it's sweet of you to offer, but no thank you, Julian. I think Tilly and I are going to go across the street and have a cup of coffee. I'm planning to convince her to join the Rights for Every Human Organization," Edna replies with a sly smile.

"I-I-I'll help y-you ladies cross the r-r-road safely," Tom offers.

The group starts to break up, Tom leading the ladies to the crosswalk and Paulina trailing behind Rodney as he heads for his car. I watch as Julian heads down the stairs, probably on his way to the bus stop. He doesn't look back and wave.

I really wish he would.

Chapter 10—Monday

WE'RE IN our usual positions, stretched out on my bed and the spare bed, a notebook on my lap and my old computer on his.

Holding my breath, I wait for Hughie's response to the first three hundred words of my Practice Common Application essay assignment for Junior College Level English. I struggle in this class but not because I can't grasp the material. It's just that sometimes I have trouble focusing. Hughie is nothing if not brutally honest when it comes to essay critiques, and I'm nothing if not desperate to get a decent grade seeing as my last essay grade suffered from a lack of effort, due to my temporary fixation with fruit juice tie-dyeing.

Side note: It takes about ten cups of fruit juice dye—three cups of crushed berries, boiled in ten cups of water and then strained—to make enough dye for a single T-shirt. Don't try to get away with less or you'll end up with light patches where you least want them. And patience is a necessary virtue when it comes to fruit juice tie-dyeing—be ready to spend some serious time in the kitchen—as you need to let the shirt soak for twenty-four hours if you want a rich color.

The best thing about fruit juice tie-dyeing is wearing the final product of your labor. Talk about DIY pride—it doesn't get better than wearing a T-shirt *you* dyed purple! The second-best thing about fruit juice tie-dyeing is that you can drink the leftover dye rather than flushing it down the toilet.

"What do you think—does it hook you by the upper lip and drag you in to shore?"

"*Hello,* Crunchy, aren't you a vegetarian? I don't think *fishing metaphors* are appropriate here." Honestly, I'm relieved that he's responding. Lately Hughie has been even more detached than usual. If he grows any more withdrawn, he'll disappear. And yeah, that was *funny*.

"Uh… I was referring to catch and release fishing." Maybe he has a point about the fish thing. Nonetheless, I'm on a roll with this essay. And although my effort to keep the earth green may not be an original topic, my enthusiasm more than makes up for it. "Maybe now I should go on to say that the act of paper-throwing, when saving the life of the spider that clings to it, as opposed to my more typical practice of recycling, does not qualify as littering."

"I know… I know… because it's written right here—" Hughie pokes at the paper my essay is scribbled on with such force I fear he'll rip it.

"You need to deal with your anger issues, dude, and not by taking it out on my essay," I warn. I need that paper.

He ignores me and starts to read aloud. "My oath to the earth: I, Kale Oswald, refuse to assault the earth with the casual and haphazard scattering of waste."

"That's right…." Hearing my words coming out of Hughie's mouth is a heady experience, even if Hughie isn't reading with sufficient expression. Soon I'm scribbling down new ideas that I don't want to fall out of my brain, which could happen if, say, I become curious about the constitution of a fresh veggie burger.

I mean, what makes a bunch of vegetables stick together like ground beef?

"I just don't get how your mind works, Crunchy."

The feeling is more than mutual.

Somehow I manage to stifle the remark *and* keep my mind on business. "You don't have to *understand* me to tell me that I nailed it with the essay, dude."

"Um… yeah. It's not too bad." Without offering the expected litany of "Crunchy Kale's Crimes against Grammar," which under normal circumstances, Hughie would enjoy delivering, he folds my essay into a paper airplane and shoots it at me.

When it crashes into my forehead, I see a rare expression of satisfaction on my brosin's face. I don't let it distract me. "I think I'm going to continue with my philosophy on plant life."

"You mean *the actual life of plants,* don't you?" When I nod, his jaw drops, which is comforting because this is Hughie being Hughie. But still, he has not been his usual goofy self since we had lunch with Aunt Serenity last weekend.

"How's this? 'Plant life, in my humble opinion, has as much of a right to an undisturbed existence as the animal, the insect, and the human being. Needless to say, I never pick a flower from the garden since I believe that, when violently uprooted, plants feel pain as surely as people do.'"

Side note: New research on the intelligence of plant life suggests that plants collect sensory data, somehow grasp its meaning, and are able to respond. They can sense things such as gravity and sound and the presence of water, and can react in ways that benefit them. Makes you feel better about singing to your plants to help 'em grow, doesn't it?

Before Hughie even has a chance to close his mouth, Dad pokes his head into my bedroom. "Hugh, your friend is here. Should I send him to your room?"

Since it's *my* room, *I* reply to my father. "Hughie has a friend?"

"I'm just doing a project with this kid…." He sounds defensive, but his explanation makes sense.

"Yeah, Dad. Go ahead and send him in." Like I said, it's *my* room.

"Mom is spending the evening with her weight-loss hypnotist, but she left slice-and-bake chocolate chip cookie dough in the refrigerator for a snack. She wants them to be gone by the time she gets home, you know, to alleviate temptation. Want me to bake cookies?"

As usual, Hughie shrugs, but I'm in the mood for warm almost-homemade cookies, so I say, "Sure, why not?"

I unfold the paper-airplane-essay and add my new ideas to the page while Hughie makes room on the spare bed for his project partner.

A minute later, I hear soft footsteps on the rug. "Hey, Hughie."

My dreadlocks stand on end—well, not literally, but it makes for a good visual—because I know that voice.

To play it cool, or not to play it cool? That is the question.

I stare at my essay. I'm going with cool.

"What's up, Julian?" Hughie pats the place beside him on the bed. "Sit down."

Julian doesn't move. "Kale? I didn't know you were Hughie's brother."

"Cousins… we're cousins," I mumble, then let my eyes pop off the messy writing on the paper in front of me to check out the boy and his lips. "Hi, Julian. *I* didn't know you and Hughie were friends." He looks fantastic again… or maybe as usual. He's dressed from head to toe in black, bringing the term *classy* to life once again tonight.

"We're partners in a project," Hughie insists, making it clear to me that he and Julian are *not* friends. I'm not sure why proving this is so important to him.

It kills me to do it, because there's nothing I'd like more than to invite Julian to sit on *my* bed and kick back with *me* for a while, but I tell them, "Well, don't let me distract you guys. I have to focus on this essay, anyway." I drag my gaze from Julian's intoxicating lips and try to sink back into the headspace of a plant in pain.

Without so much as a "hi, how are ya?" my brosin and Julian get down to business. I have no problem ignoring their discussion, since FDR is of zero interest to me. Hippies didn't even exist back when he was president, as far as I know.

After about thirty minutes, Dad knocks on the door and then comes in holding a sturdy double-layer paper plate of warm chocolate chip cookies and a roll of paper towels. Incidentally, the Oswalds are no longer napkin/facial tissue people since Mom's recent philosophy is that paper towels and toilet paper can get the same jobs done with "more strength and style" and less time spent at the grocery store, which seems to be her least favorite place to shop these days. He sticks the plate on my desk.

"Now don't you boys work too hard, you hear?" Dad's advice is embarrassing. "You know what they say about all work and no play?"

"Thank you, Mr. Oswald. The cookies smell great." I stop mid eye roll, as Julian's attitude toward Dad takes me by surprise. Gone is the defiant teen. He has been replaced by an angelic choirboy.

Dad smiles at Julian and says, "I like your friend, Hughie. Nice kid."

"We're just partners in a history project," Hughie mumbles. "Not friends."

Before Dad leaves the room, he glances back and says, "Hey, Julian, want me to bring you a package of bacon bits to sprinkle on top of the cookies? The combination creates this contrasting burst of sweet and salty flavor that's tough to describe in words, but is oh, so good."

I glance across the room at Hughie, hoping to catch his attention. A mutual, annoyed eye roll would be satisfying right about now. But his eyes are glued to my old computer.

"You know, Mr. Oswald, I'm happy with the cookies just as they are. But I appreciate the offer. Maybe next time." Julian is a diplomatic choirboy.

"Have it your way, then. But you have no idea what you're missing. Pop-quiz time, boys: 'Have it your way' is a vintage slogan for which fast food chain?"

Hughie and I both know the answer is Burger King. Dad has drilled the *Have It Your Way* Burger King jingle into our heads. And usually Hughie can't get enough of Dad's retro-burger humor and is chomping at the bit to answer pop-quiz questions before I do. Tonight he just shrugs.

"I'm extremely disappointed. I thought one of you would know the answer, after all of the effort I put into teaching you boys the important things in life...." Dad walks out of the room, shaking his head.

He looked defeated, but I'm still in the mood for cookies. I stop working on my essay to grab a few while they're warm. Julian and Hughie are too socially awkward to put their FDR project aside while they eat. I listen in to their discussion.

"So we're gonna go with me playing the part of the reporter, and you being FDR, right?" Hughie asks.

Julian nods and takes a bite of a cookie. Not that I'm looking at his mouth. Again.

"And just in case I'm not at school on Friday for the presentation, I'm going to print out my questions and cut them up and glue them onto notecards. Then you can get another kid in the class to read them and you can respond, just like we planned."

Julian looks confused. "Do you feel like you're coming down with a flu or something? So you might not be in school on Friday?" He asks what I want to know.

"Nah, it's nothing like that. *Just in case,* is what I said…. You know, it's best to be prepared." Hughie is acting like a loon.

"Okay, I guess." And just like that, the two of them get back to the New Deal.

I'm left to wonder about my brosin's confusing words. He hasn't missed a day of school all year, except for when he was living under the bridge. And yeah, it was an odd thing to say, but then, Hughie's kind of odd. So I dismiss it.

When Hughie goes to Dad's office to use the printer, Julian stands up and packs his messenger bag with notebooks. I'm extremely aware that I'm alone in the room with Julian and his spectacular lips, of which the top one is sporting a smudge of chocolate. For some reason that I suspect has a lot to do with my inexplicable urge to lick the chocolate off his lip, my palms start to sweat. But since I'm easily distracted, *my* attention is caught by how *Julian's* attention is caught by the few remaining chocolate chip cookies on the paper plate. He seems to be as obsessed with them as I was with the concept of fruit juice tie-dye back in early January.

"Go ahead, dude. Finish them off," I tell him.

"Uh… I was kinda wondering if I could wrap them up and take them home. My mom… she loves this kind of cookie."

Weird. I catch myself before I say it and rip off a few paper towels. "Here, wrap them up in these."

"Thanks."

I want Julian to look at me instead of the cookies. I want to see if I can read what's going on in his dark eyes, but then, as he wraps up the cookies, he licks away the chocolate smudge, and I'm distracted in a whole new way. And yes, I'm fully aware that I'm a piece of work.

Hughie comes back into my room and, without a word, hands Julian some papers. With cookies and papers and messenger bag in hand, Julian tells him, "I gotta head out—the last bus to East and Fifth leaves in ten minutes."

Hughie dismisses Julian with a nod. I'm going to have to talk to him about his embarrassing lack of manners, but something more pressing is on my mind. *East Street and Fifth Avenue....* It hits me that Julian lives near the intersection with the Global Village Coffee Shop. I could sure go for a late-night cup of coffee. But again, I fight the urge to offer him a ride home. I try to avoid being rejected whenever possible. It's bad for the fragile hippie ego.

Chapter 11—Thursday

Julian, noon

I LITERALLY bump into Kale at lunch on Thursday—or actually, my tray knocks into his. He freaks out momentarily, looking all around to see who may have caught our lunch trays engaging in intimate physical contact, and when he realizes that it's our little secret, he resumes staring at my mouth. He does this a lot.

"Hi, Julian." After a couple of seconds, he pulls his eyes off my lips to look down at my tray, where my milk carton lies on its side as a result of our little accident. "You eating alone again, dude?"

For a split second, I think he's gonna invite me to sit with him. But then he checks around us again, probably feeling trapped and/or targeted when publicly in my fancy-ass company, so I just shrug. He doesn't care who I eat with or if I even eat. Kale Oswald might be cute, but he's a poser. In fact, he's a poser of the worst kind, pretending to be a human rights advocate in order to fill blank spaces on the Common App.

"Did you finish making the video on the crosswalk timing?" he asks, looking around yet again, his eyes lingering on the table where his friends are sitting. They haven't noticed Kale interacting with "the faggot" yet.

"Yeah. I'm gonna bring it to REHO tomorrow night so everybody can watch it on my computer. I already dropped a copy by the Crestdale City Office of Transportation, just so they can be aware of the problem before we make a formal request to extend the time." Ah, his buddies have caught on to the fact that he's talking to me. And they're gawking at us. Pointing even. This conversation is close to its end.

"Sounds good... I... um...." The poser is at a loss for words, having realized our interaction has been outed.

I suppose I'll let him off the hook, seeing as he looks about as uncomfortable as a pig at a bacon-bits packaging plant. I turn toward my usual empty table, but as I walk away from him, I remember something. "Is Hughie sick?" I ask, looking over my shoulder.

Kale is still standing there looking kind of tortured. "Not that I know of."

"He hasn't been in class today."

It's Kale's turn to shrug. "That's weird. Dad dropped us both off at school this morning."

He doesn't seem overly concerned about MIA Hughie, so I say, "Well, tell him to text me tonight so we can go over the final details of our project." We're considering wearing costumes.

"Will do." We both retreat to our opposite sides of the caf. I'm thinking about how, despite his shallowness, his cascade of yellow dreadlocks is adorable, whereas he's probably thinking how strange I am, because I'm wearing a matching necklace and earrings set from the dollar store. *Whatever.*

Kale, 10:00 p.m.

DAD IS freaking out. Freaking out so much he actually called Mom at her henna tattooing appointment to see if *she'd* heard from Hughie. And he knows Mom can't tolerate being interrupted while having a henna design applied to her hands. She says it's supposed to be a steady, mystical experience.

It was a daring move on Dad's part. Commendable, though probably unnecessary.

He comes into my bedroom and starts to pace in the space between the beds. "Hughie hasn't contacted your mother *or* your aunt. Neither of them have any idea where the boy is."

"Maybe he has a date." We both know that this is a ridiculous suggestion. I snicker.

"This is not a funny situation, Kalin. Your cousin is missing. He never came home from school, and he hasn't contacted any of us with an explanation." Dad rubs his palm over his head and then back down over his face. "It just isn't like him not to be here, especially since he knew I was making my special pulled pork for dinner tonight."

I wrinkle my nose. "You're right. Wild horses couldn't drag him away from your pulled pork sandwiches."

Dad flops down onto the bed that Hughie sleeps on. The bed he sleeps on like, every night since last October right after the Filmore Bridge incident.

I guess it wouldn't kill me to call it Hughie's bed.

"Concentrate for a minute, son—did he tell you he had any out-of-the-ordinary plans tonight? The library, maybe?"

I shake my head for the zillionth time. "No. You dropped us off in front of the school and I went to homeroom. I figured he did the same."

He sighs and the sound makes him seem old and tired and worn out. I feel guilty, and I'm not sure why.

Something hits me. "But that kid Julian who came over here to study last week told me Hughie wasn't in class today."

My father shoots up off the bed. I had no idea that a man with such a large beef-belly could be so agile. "He wasn't in school today? Interesting. I think I'm going to try to get in touch with Mary Pat again to see if the school contacted her."

I start to shrug in the "I wish I could help you but I haven't got a clue, dude" way, but midshrug something else hits me. What if he took a bus over to Julian's house to study? They have that FDR project due tomorrow, and God knows, those two nerds are all about having the best project in the class. They're probably doing something geeky like picking out costumes. *Ha!*

I grab my peacoat and throw it on over my plaid flannel sleep pants and T-shirt. Then I slide my bare feet into the Birki's beside my bedroom door and head down the stairs. Dad's talking on the phone, and is in such an intense conversation that I figure he won't even realize I left. On one hand, I don't want to get his hopes up that I'm about to find Hughie, but on the other hand, I don't want to worry him that he lost me too, so I scribble a BRB note on the whiteboard in the hallway, pull his keys off the hook, and slip out the door.

Dad has a much sportier vehicle than Mom. *Not.* He has a royal blue Nissan Cube. It's almost impossible to keep a low profile while driving a neon-colored rolling box, but I nonetheless start it up and head across town. Added bonus to this brosin-finding mission: I'm in the mood for organic coffee.

Kale, 10:30 p.m.

LUCKY FOR me the Global Village Coffee Shop is open until eleven. I walk in slowly—a footloose hippie in his natural habitat—and head for the bar.

"Kale!"

I know that voice. Except for Hughie going missing, this night is turning out better than I hoped. Now I won't have to stalk the long row of dated duplexes near this address, trying to figure out where the Mendez family lives. "Hey, Julian."

"Come over here." Julian is sitting alone in a corner booth, his computer in front of him, books and notebooks stacked on either side, a mug of coffee in his hand. "You forgot to tell Hughie to call me. I haven't heard from him all night."

My heart sinks a little because I'm not going to be able to deliver good news to Dad. "So Hughie's not here with you?"

Julian shakes his head.

"He's not in the men's room, maybe?"

"Um… *no.* I just told you I haven't heard from him."

When I drop into the booth across from Julian, my cool hippie exterior slips a bit. Then I sigh, and it sounds tired and worn like my father's sigh did. Maybe tonight *isn't* going as well as I thought.

"What's the matter?" Julian closes his laptop. "What's going on?"

"It's Hughie. I think he might be gone."

"Gone like… *dead*?" Julian's eyes get round.

"Well, no. Gone, as in, I think he might have run away from… from *my* home." And *his* home—it was his home too. So I clarify. "I think he ran away from home."

"He has been acting *off* in our classes all week."

"Acting *off*—in what way?" I hadn't noticed Hughie acting too much weirder than usual. In fact, this week, Hughie has been what he always is to me—a slightly eclectic, mostly silent addition to my bedroom furniture. A dark cloud of guilt blows across the Global Village and parks itself right over my head.

"Well, it started when he got me all prepared to present the AP US History project by myself. In case he, by some chance, wasn't at school on Friday. Who prepares their project partner for his *possible* absence?"

"He said something about that on Monday, right?" I scrape the dusty back of my brain for details but don't come up with much.

"Maybe he knew he was gonna be gone by Friday."

I must be completely clueless because that bright idea never crossed my mind. Until now, when a relative stranger points it out to me. The guilt cloud settles lower on my head.

"Plus, all week, he looked worried and bothered… like something was big-time wrong. Know what I mean?"

To be perfectly honest, I didn't notice any of that. Hughie just sat silently, night after night, on the spare bed—okay, on *his* bed—with my old computer—okay, *his* computer—propped on his knees, eyes glued to the screen. I figured he was studying. "I didn't notice anything out of the ordinary."

"You didn't notice that he looked pale and nervous? Shit, I even caught the kid trembling a couple times." He shakes his head. "Wake up and smell the coffee, Kale."

I could laugh, seeing as we're in a coffee shop, but I don't because I'm getting a serious case of the guilts here, which is a new thing for me. "Well, maybe I noticed a little bit." I'm *so* lying. When Julian looks up at me and tilts his head, I can tell he knows.

This is when it hits me. Maybe *clueless* is the wrong word to describe me; maybe the adjective is a lot less pleasant than *clueless*. Like self-absorbed… or insensitive. Or both.

"So where do you think he ran to?" Julian asks. And since I need to focus on *anything* other than how personally responsible I am for what's happened to Hughie, I concentrate on Julian. There's something different about him tonight—about how he looks—and it isn't his lips. It's his eyes. He's definitely wearing that stuff girls wear on their eyelashes… mascara, I think it's called. Because tonight his eyelashes are thick and they curl up, making his eyes look a little bit too wide open. And so pretty. Julian's eyes, I decide, are every bit as spectacular as his lips.

But this admission is neither here nor there when it comes to my brosin, Hughie's, disappearance. "I don't have a clue where he went." I'm pretty sure I just said these exact words to my Dad. *Ugh*—more guilt.

"Think, Kale. *Think*—has something been bothering him lately?"

"How should I know?"

"Um, *hello*! You share a bedroom with Hughie. You must *talk* to him."

I look back at Julian with what I'm certain is a totally blank face. *Holy crap—Hughie and I don't talk much, do we?*

"You've got to be kidding me." Julian opens his computer. "Well, good luck finding him. I'd say you've got your work cut out for you."

But I'm not quite as oblivious as I may seem. "There is *something* that has been bothering him lately."

Julian slowly lifts his eyes from the screen and waits for me to continue, but he doesn't look like he has much confidence in my ability to identify Hughie's problem.

Still, I cut through the thick cloud of guilt that's starting to suffocate me and spill the only reason I can think of that Hughie would run. "It's about his mother. Me and Hughie had lunch with her last weekend and she told us she wanted him to go back to living with her."

"I take it Hughie doesn't like that idea."

I shake my head, remembering the bummed-out expression on Hughie's face when Aunt Serenity informed him that she wanted "her sugar bear" to move back into "his momsie bear's" apartment. "No, he doesn't like the idea at all."

Julian seems to think that there's more I need to say, so he holds his tongue.

Bummed-out—wrong term for the look on Hughie's face. Try appalled, or horrified, maybe. These SAT words work much better to describe the green eyes that bulged in panic over freckled cheeks that looked a little bit too pasty to be a positive sign. Not to mention pale lips that stretched down and out in an "oh my freaking God" grimace. There is only one conclusion I can make: I sure missed the boat on how distressed my brosin was at lunch that day.

"Hughie is happy living with us. He doesn't want to leave." I'd never before really thought about what living with us meant to Hughie. I'm pretty sure I should have.

"Jeez." Julian recognizes my cluelessness in the face of Hughie's desperation with another shake of his head. "That could've been the reason he took off. He was probably scared he was gonna be forced to go back to her."

I nod but can't speak. *I literally can't*. It's all I can do to ride the wave of sudden awareness that's flooding my brain. Bubbles of perspiration pop out on my temples and stream down the sides of my face. I don't even care if Julian sees me sweat.

"Where would he go, Kale?" Julian reaches out and tries to pull me out of my tsunami of sudden realization, so I can do some rational thinking. "I mean, if he was trying to avoid being sent back to her, where would he go?"

I wipe my dripping forehead with my sleeve and admit, "I'm not sure, but I'm gonna figure it out." I consider tacking on "dude" to the end of the sentence, but I don't. For some reason, I just don't.

Julian, 10:30 p.m.

ON THE night I met Kale in the basement of the Community House, I thought, "this guy is easy on the eyes," but to be real, his expression did nothing to draw me in. *Nada.* Pretty blue eyes, check that box. But did his expression reflect that he was a dependable and empathetic ally in the fight for human rights for all people? I couldn't check that box because I never fully bought his dedication to anything but coming off as chill—not when I met him at REHO and not when I saw him at school. For the most part, he was just present, in body but not in spirit. Maybe he cracked a bit when I spilled my sob story at the Gay-Straight Alliance, but he got right back to staring blankly. I wonder how he would have reacted had he known I was attending the GSA as a straight transgender girl, rather than what he assumed, as a gay boy. I fight not to roll my eyes.

Right now, though, his genuine humanity is peeking through the clouds of self-absorption. Not that he's particularly comfortable with this new development, because at the moment Kale is pacing back and forth past my booth in the coffee shop. And he's practically drowning in his own sweat.

"I've got to figure out what to do...." He's mumbling shit I don't think I'm meant to hear. "I need to find him before...."

"Sit down, Kale. You're wearing out the rug."

He stops and looks down at the tired oriental beneath his Birkenstocks.

"Sit down, and we'll think this thing through." Serious thinking requires a man bun, or it would if I was, indeed, a man. In any case, I pull my hair up on top of my head and fasten it there with the elastic on my wrist so it stops getting in my eyes. "Why is it that Hughie doesn't wanna live with his mother?"

Kale takes a few minutes to weigh and measure. I can see it in his eyes. He's asking himself, "can a dude who wears mascara be trustworthy?"

He finally nods, as if he's decided that I'm worthy to learn the family secrets, whether or not I'm wearing makeup. "Hughie's mom isn't the typical mother, you know?"

I shake my head. "*My* mother is three hundred pounds, half-Dominican and half-Filipino, and she's pretty old—sixty-one, if you must know. She isn't your typical mom either, but I wouldn't trade her... and I wouldn't want to live with anybody else. So, to me, a mom doesn't have to be typical to be amazing."

"Well, *I* haven't seen *my* mother all week thanks to a white sale at the Factory Outlet Stores in Wellburg. Did you know there's a

Bedroom, Bathroom, and Yonder, as well as a Linens Are Love and a Beddy-Bye Magic for Tots, all in the same strip of the outlet mall? Well, I do, because it's all Mom has talked about for ten days!" In response to my shrug, he adds, "Kathy Oswald isn't exactly your average mother either, is all I'm saying."

Not only is Kale apparently struggling with regret, but he's also fuming. I've never seen this side of him. "So we all have pretty out-there moms—what's the big deal with Hughie's mother that makes him not want to live with her?"

Still standing on the rug in front of the table, he starts rotating his hips, shimmying his shoulders, and seductively pulling up his T-shirt. "See what I'm saying?" he asks, still in motion.

I rub my eyes. My best guess is that an insect of some variety is crawling up Kale's leg and across his chest. "Um… not so much."

After dropping the hem of his shirt in frustration, Kale leans over, sticks his elbows on the table, and confides in a hushed tone, "Julian, Hughie's mother is a stripper."

"Oh. Now, I see." But maybe I really *don't* see, because being a stripper doesn't make her a bad person.

"*Do you?*"

"Unless she's a paint stripper, I think I do."

He rolls his eyes. "She works full-time at the Dance Dirty for Me Lounge."

"Okay, okay… I get the picture. But being an exotic dancer doesn't make her a sucky mother. So why doesn't he want to live with her? Does she… like, *take her work home,* if you catch my drift?"

Kale straightens up and shrugs. "I don't think she gets paid, you know, for the times when her 'guy friends' sleep over. But they sleep over *a lot*. And Aunt Serenity is all about herself—she never listens to what Hughie says about *anything*." Kale speaks slowly, as if he's being hit hard by every word that leaves his mouth. Like maybe he's noticing how much he has in common with his self-consumed aunt.

"I can only imagine." Actually, I *can't* imagine how Hughie has managed to do so well in school. There must have been a lot of very distracting background noise while he tried to study. "And I agree that we need to find him."

"If he's not in school tomorrow, let's meet up at the end of the day in the caf and figure something out," Kale suggests.

"I can be there. And I'll bring Anna and Kandy. They'll help too." They're volunteers of the highest caliber. I know this from personal experience.

"Okay… but be warned—I highly doubt that Hughie's going to be in school to help with your US History presentation in the morning."

"That's all right. I can handle it myself, and I'll bring home a good grade for both of us." I start to pack my books and notebooks into my messenger bag. "You think your dad will call the police?" Kale is quiet while he thinks over my question, which I'd assumed he'd answer with an automatic "of course he will."

"Hughie's been in trouble before—you know, he's run away a whole bunch of times. I seriously doubt that Dad will go straight to the police with this. I think instead he'll keep it quiet and try to find Hughie himself first."

I've never before had the opportunity to witness a person being tossed unceremoniously into the hard, cold reality of the cruel world, but it's literally happening before my very eyes. Kale is realizing that there are kids who have it hard in life, and some who have it incredibly hard.

"I'm pretty sure Dad will give it a few days. He'll try to treat it as a private family matter, unless Hughie stays… gone."

Once my messenger bag is packed, I stand up beside Kale. "You gonna grab a cup of coffee for the road?" The café workers are wiping down the machines, and soon coffee will no longer be an option.

Kale shakes his head before I finish asking the question. "No. I lost my taste for coffee tonight." Kale walks out of the café, still shaking his head.

A different boy left the Global Village Coffee Shop than had entered it thirty minutes earlier.

CHAPTER 12—FRIDAY

Kale, 6:45 a.m.

SOMETHING IS wrong with my bowl of granola this morning. The crunch—it just isn't the same. There's something missing.

I know for a fact that the granola isn't stale. I just peeled the cover off a new can ten minutes ago. I heard the distinctive pop of the safety seal. No, this granola is as fresh as the morning dew. Or a daisy. Whatever—it is very, very fresh.

Maybe it's the almond milk. But a whiff of the container satisfies me: the almond milk is as fresh as the granola. And similarly fresh is the honey I drizzled over the top of the granola and almond milk.

The only thing different about breakfast this morning is that there's no Hughie gawking at me over his omelet as I inform him of the wonders of raw honey.

Side note: Raw honey is the sweet liquid honeybees make from concentrated flower nectar. It has not been heated, pasteurized, or processed in any way, shape, or form. Incidentally, honeybees are the only insect that makes food people eat. And yes, honeybees do sting, but you'd have to be stung over a thousand times for it to be fatal. I consider that to be good news, seeing as, if I got stung in the process of relocating a bee from my bathroom window, I'd be in little danger of dying.

The worst part of this morning is that it's so quiet. It's true that Hughie never said too much, but it still seems silent without him here.

What is happening to my crunchy life?

Before I have an opportunity to ponder the question, Dad comes into the kitchen and plunks himself down across from me in what is usually Hughie's seat.

"No baco-saus-eggs omelet?" I tease, but it's halfhearted.

Normally, Dad makes a couple of omelets each morning that consist of contributions from the entire barnyard. Ham and bacon and sausage links, of course, but he also scrambles some steak into the eggs that hold the hearty meat-blend together. Sometimes over breakfast, he and Hughie debate a subject such as the best cut of beef to grill for a crowd, as they consume their meat-laden omelet. Other times, they poke fun at people who eat tofu as a meat alternative. Yeah, they tease me, but it's all in fun. And, for the most part, I can take it.

"Not this morning, Kalin."

My name is Kale. I just think it, though.

"It's my fault Hughie's run away." After this declaration, Dad's head sinks into his hands. "It's my fault he's out in the cold right now."

"Dad—it's not your fault. We both know that Hughie takes off whenever he's… when things aren't going his way." That came out wrong. It sounded like I blame him, when I need to shoulder some of the burden for this disaster.

"I should've made his living situation with us permanent a long time ago, son. Instead, I let the kid live here, feeling like a perpetual houseguest. Sure, I fed him the best steaks and cuts of pork loin that money can buy, but he never became a *real* part of this family. He left because he didn't trust that I'd protect him."

Knife to the gut. I acted the same way. "We'll find him, Dad. And when we do, we can make things right."

Dad lifts his head from his hands but looks past me at the picture of the three Oswalds—Dad, Mom, and me. "I thought you didn't want a little brother."

His words aren't intended as an accusation, but nonetheless, they are.

Had I made that fact so crystal clear?

Instead of challenging his statement, I again assure him, "We'll find Hughie and fix things. No worries." It's starting to dawn on me how much I need this to be true.

Dad looks at me, even more surprised. "Well, that's good to hear." He stares into my eyes for a second, like he's in a daze. Then he clears his throat. "I'm hesitant to go to the police, you know. He ran away so often when he lived with Mary Pat...." The name "Serenity" is as far gone as Hughie is.

Hughie ran away from various apartments where he lived with Aunt Mary Pat so many times that Dad took pity on him. Short visits to our house turned into this semistable, never openly discussed, completely informal, "temporary but then again not" living situation for Hughie. "What do you think the police will do if they find out he ran again?"

"I think they'll place him in foster care, or more likely, because of his age, he'll.... Hughie will probably end up in a group home. One that's far from here."

And just like that, Sam Oswald of *Oh, Tires!* is crying. Sure, his head has dropped back into his hands so I can't see his eyes, but I know the signs—the sniffling, the shaky breathing, the wetness on the kitchen table—he's crying for sure. And at this moment, I make a startling realization: I'm crying too.

Julian, 3:00 p.m.

I HAVE the best volunteer friends in the universe.

Anna and Kandy have actually brainstormed a list of ideas regarding how to:
locate Hughie
let Hughie know he's not alone in the world, which is their specialty
bring Hughie home
"Hey, ladies, have I told you lately that I love you?" I wink as if I'm joking, but I'm not.

Kandy approaches me first. "As a matter of fact, no. We're sorely deprived of expressions of your love, Julian." She can't hold back laughter, but I can't make myself laugh.

Anna hugs me. "We've got some great ideas to help Hughie. Kale's meeting us too, right?"

I look down at my wrist, as if I were wearing a watch. "I'd say he's... like five minutes late. Let's give him hell!"

"Yeah, sounds like a plan—kick the kid when he's down!" Kandy quips and reaches into the pocket of her skirt. "Here, check out our list...."

Anna and I huddle close to Kandy to look at the list of ideas about how to bring Hughie home.

"Hey, guys." Kale turns the corner from the hallway and heads into the caf. There's something different about him that I can't put a finger on. Maybe he simply didn't get enough sleep last night, and his lack of energy and sullen expression are actually exhaustion. "Thanks for showing up."

Anna and Kandy look at each other, and through their unique brand of silent communication Anna gets the go-ahead to be the first to speak. "Of course we showed up—why wouldn't we?"

"Your cousin needs to come home, and we're going to do everything we can to help," Kandy adds. As always, the volunteers are on the exact same page.

Kale stops a few feet from us. Maybe he's afraid their compassion is contagious and will end up inconveniencing him and his effort to be hip. "Why do you guys care so much, anyway?" he asks, his eyes narrow.

Anna gasps, which is such an innocent-Anna thing to do. Kandy touches her arm, and they exchange another one of those meaningful glances, but they manage to hold their tongues. I'm not as PC. "Nice way to be appreciative, Oswald."

Kale turns to look at me. "I just don't get why these girls are investing their time and energy in finding my cousin. Do they even *know* Hughie?" He drops his backpack to the floor. "But I get why *you* want him back in school, Julian. You probably need him to help you survive all the group projects in your brainiac classes."

I'm tempted to bitch-slap him and then turn around and strut away, but I know better than anybody else that sometimes people in pain lash out. "Chill, will you? We all want Hughie to come back so he can pick up where he left off.... You know, so he can hit the books hard and be the valedictorian of Crestdale High School, like he deserves. Let's find him and bring him home."

"Nice thought, but the sad truth is—Hughie doesn't have a home." Kale is more argumentative than I've ever seen him. "That's the root of the problem. Staying with us was just a 'temporary thing.'"

"Let's take a seat and talk this out," Anna suggests, as always looking for a way to calm things down.

"Hughie's best chance comes from him having some people in his corner. And that'll be us." Kandy heads toward the only cafeteria table that hasn't been pushed up against the wall. "Come on." She tugs on Kale's arm.

The four of us walk across the caf and sit down on top of the table, our feet resting on the attached bench. Since I'm the single unifying factor in this stressed-out little party, I figure it's my job to get the ball rolling. "I mentioned to Anna and Kandy before school that you think Hughie ran away because he's afraid his mother is going to force him to live with her again. And that her home isn't a good environment for a kid."

The new superserious, guilt-tripping version of Kale is gazing out the glass wall in the back of the caf. There's a bit of snow in the courtyard from a midday snowfall, but it's more or less just a cold, gray day. I figure Kale's worrying that his cousin is somewhere outside, cold and alone.

"He's been staying with your family since... since when, Kale?" I ask to bring him into the conversation. But he still looks distracted, like his mind is wandering in and out of every potential hiding spot in the city. I repeat my question. "How long has Hughie been staying with you?"

"Since last October—at least he's been with us full-time since then. That was a bad month for him, and when we found him, he was half-frozen and beat up... and hanging out with homeless people." I guess I wasn't the only Crestdale High School junior who was struggling with life last fall. "But it's never been an *official* thing. It's like he's always just 'visiting' our home, but nobody knows exactly how long he's going to be visiting for." Kale is more up-front with his private family business than I figured he'd be.

Anna reaches over and touches Kale's arm. "It sounds like a pretty awkward situation." He stares at her hand on his arm like it's stuff that dripped from a toddler's nose.

"Where does Hughie *want* to live?" Kandy asks, trying to focus our small group on business.

Kale sighs, and it makes him seem like he's forty years old. *Yeah, ancient.* "With us—all Hughie wants is to live with us."

"Why haven't your parents adopted him, or something like that?" Anna asks sweetly. I've been meaning to ask him this, as well. "Doing that may have solved this problem before it even happened, right?"

"I don't think my dad wanted to piss off his little sister. She's Hughie's mother."

The girls nod, and I think I get it too. "You're pretty sure he wasn't… like… abducted?" This isn't an easy question for me to ask, but it needs to be voiced.

"I mean, I can't say definitely no, but Hughie has a long history of running away."

"A long history?"

"Uh-huh. He ran away from home twelve times before he came to stay with us."

"Where did he go when he ran away?" Kandy asks the obvious question.

"Different places. He was picked up by the police for loitering at the Sinking Stone Mall twice, and in the movie theater in Tilton once. And another time they found him in a bust at a crack house sort of place. He was sleeping in an upstairs bedroom under a pile of coats." Kale is counting off the instances of his cousin's escapes on his fingers. "Me and Dad found him in an ATM lobby at a downtown bank one time, and two other times, in the summer, we found him in the bathrooms at a couple of different rest areas on the highway. And the other times he was staying under the Filmore Bridge."

"Under the Filmore Bridge?" Kandy perks up. "Our church used to go down there every month. We'd set up a soup kitchen in a tent and feed the homeless youth. There were a whole bunch of them. It was really sad."

I wonder what those kids had to do to survive. It's probably not pretty, and also not something I want to dwell on because I know that if Mama had tossed me out for being transgender, I could have been one of them.

"Do you think he went back to the bridge this time?" Anna asks.

Kale shakes his head. "No, Dad said they fenced it off so the kids can't get under there anymore."

"Where should we start, then?" Kandy, like always, is eager to set a plan in motion. "How about we check the mall?"

"Maybe the arcade by the food court," I suggest because if I had nowhere to go, I might go there so I'd be warm and dry and I wouldn't have to be alone.

"I've got my mother's minivan. You guys can pile in, and I'll drive us over there." Kale glances at me. "We're going to end up missing REHO tonight. Are you cool with that, Julian?"

"It's not a problem. Just swing by the Community House, and I'll drop off the video I made."

He nods. "I can do that."

We slide off the table, but for a minute we all stand here staring at each other. Maybe we're waiting for some expression of gratitude, but Kale offers none. He just heads toward the cafeteria's side door and we follow along behind him.

Kale, 10:00 p.m.

"KALIN, WHERE have you been?" My father is sitting alone at the kitchen table, staring toward the window that overlooks the dark backyard... at nothing.

Dad's staring at nothing....

"At the mall. And the movies."

"Your cousin is missing and you went out to have fun with your friends?"

I sniff the air and it smells like tacos. Beef tacos, to be specific. "Well, Dad, your nephew is missing and you had a Mexican Meat Fiesta."

"I thought the smell might draw Hughie home," Dad replies, his voice breaking. "It didn't work. I packed all the meat away in the fridge."

I feel bad for throwing Dad under the bus, but I was just living by my long-held philosophy that the best defense is a good offense. "Sorry. And I wasn't having fun… me and my friends were at the movie theater and the mall looking for Hughie."

Dad stands up and pulls me into his arms. "I'm sorry too, son." He chokes, and I'm forced to admit that Sam Oswald is crying again. "I'm just so worried about him. I don't know what to do."

"Did you talk to Mary Pat about it?" It's time to call a spade a spade, and that means calling Aunt Serenity by her given name. "Is she upset?"

Dad lets me go and points to the chair beside his. We sit down. "If she's upset, she didn't show it. Mary Pat went to work tonight. She said to leave a message on her phone if he came back."

"Oh, that kind of sucks. What about Mom? What did she say?"

Dad takes me by surprise and hops up out of his seat. "Coffee, Kalin?"

"No thanks." I watch as he fills his mug. "What did Mom say?" I'm persistent, for once, when it comes to Mom's sketchy commitment to our family.

"Your mother… well, Kathy told me that she'll keep her eyes open for him… in the vicinity of her dentist's office. She has an evening appointment to… uh… well, she's having her teeth whitened tonight." He stares at the mug in his hand.

My frustration at Mom's frivolity escapes my brain through my mouth in the form of sarcasm. "That sounds like Mom. I don't know why you give her a pass on all the tough stuff, Dad." I've never before voiced this kind of complaint. My face burns, but I don't regret speaking up. Maybe *happy wife, happy life* is Dad's philosophy, but she's my mother and Hughie's aunt too, which means she has responsibilities.

"Your mother has been having a very difficult time since she lost her job. But I think the time has come for me to talk to her about how she's planning to move forward in her life."

I didn't mean to distract him from his purpose, which is to find Hughie. So I ask, "What's your plan for Hughie, Dad? Are you going to file a missing person report?"

"I should… I know I should. And if I thought for a minute that he'd been actually taken against his will I *would*. But I think he did what he's done so many times before—Hughie took off because he was afraid and he didn't trust our family enough to confide in us." Dad gulps the coffee down so fast I cringe because I'm certain he burned his throat, but he seems not to notice. "I'm afraid of what will happen if I make a report. Ours will be the second family home that he ran from, although he was technically just a guest here."

I suddenly need to be alone, which isn't one of my typical needs. Usually I need to know stuff like what ant poop looks like and if tongue prints are unique to every individual. I'm surprised by my overwhelming need for personal time and space, and my exit isn't as graceful as I'd hoped. "Gotta pee like Seabiscuit."

And I'm out of there with the speed of a racehorse.

Side note: "Pee like a racehorse." I use this expression quite frequently, so naturally I became curious about its origin. Do racehorses really pee so much? According to my research, yes, they do, and then some. Horses produce almost two gallons of pee per day. And from what I gather, when horses urinate, it's quite an impressive sight. In my research, a peeing horse has been called "dramatic" and "a spectacle." And throughout history, racehorses have commonly been given diuretics so that they pee excessively before a race. A racehorse can be ten pounds lighter after taking a leak.

My bedroom seems overly quiet, which is ridiculous since when Hughie's in here, he hardly says a word unless questioned directly. And then he delivers a guarded reply, always keeping it short and to the point. Hughie never rambles. But maybe he has stuff to say, and he shuts up because he knows that I wouldn't care about any of it. He knows that I'd say something like, "Whatevs," and resume telling him about the wonders of the Woodstock Festival.

Things need to change around here.

I need to change.

I pull off my tie-dye T-shirt and jeans, and kick off my moccasins. And here I stand. The real me.

Not so hipster at all, am I? Just a skinny sixteen-year-old boy in tighty-whities.

The time has come to take a long hard look at myself.

And how is it I know this?

An easy question to answer—it's because my guilt has grown so thick it feels like a second skin I need to shed.

I'm a hippie-imposter.

The most legendary hippies of all—John, Paul, George, and Ringo—declared in song that love is all you need. But I refused to give Hughie so much as a like. And doesn't a certain popular Beatles' tune declare that we get by with a little help from our friends? I left my cousin hanging alone in the wind. And, according to my research, hippies are comfortable living in communal dwellings; I have trouble sharing my bedroom.

I may *look* like a hippie with my dreadlocks and tie-dyed T-shirts, but I'm just an average kid who cares about stuff like being popular at school and getting accepted into a decent college. *Hippie* is the laid-back, chill identity I hide behind.

Hippie. It's really just the personal theme I've adopted so I can pass as cool and avoid having to think about who I *really* am.

Holy crap—I'm a fake! I'm the Walt Disney World Hippie Theme Park of teenage boys in Crestdale!

And maybe I have no idea who I really am, other than a guy who professed to be pro-human rights but who looked the other way at the human being in desperate need who lives in my frigging bedroom with me.

I'm drawn to the mirror above my bureau. As I stand here, it's like my fingertips grow tiny minds of their own; they start ripping away, pulling apart, and separating my dreads. But I get nowhere fast. In fact, my head has become a disaster area—a frizzy, knotted, semidreaded rat's nest.

I refuse to become more upset over my stupid hair than I am over my missing cousin. Wrapping a T-shirt around my head, I sneak down the hall. In the bathroom, Mom's toenail-scissors rest on the vanity, all shiny and silver, beckoning me. I grab them and pick out my first dreadlock victim. *Snip.* For just a moment, I wonder what to do with it—I could wrap it in toilet paper and stick it under my pillow for safekeeping—but I quickly realize this is not the answer. I toss it in the trash and move on, snipping away at Kale Oswald, the pseudohippie, dread by dread.

When I return to my room, I'm a nearly naked nonhippie with uneven, inch-long blond spikes sticking up off my head. My mushroom days are over. I have morphed into a pineapple, minus the leafy crown.

I lie down in bed, pull the covers to my chin, and turn out the light on the bedside table.

What is happening to my crunchy life?

This question is quickly replaced.

What is happening to my cousin, Hughie?

The last thing I do before I close my eyes is lift my phone from the lamp on my bedside table and send a group text to my new friends, Anna, Kandy, and Julian.

Kale: *Thanks for all the help. I appreciate it more than you know.*

Maybe I haven't the slightest clue who I am anymore, but maybe this is okay, because I'm finally being honest with myself and the world.

CHAPTER 13—SATURDAY

Julian, 10:00 a.m.

"NEXT SATURDAY, Jules, is your appointment with the endocrinologist. All your blood work will be back and you know what will happen that day, right? You'll be getting your prescriptions." Mama hasn't mastered the art of appearing bored, as I have.

She wears her worry on her wrinkled forehead and pursed lips.

And she's right. Next Saturday is a big day. Huge, even, and I'm scared, but only because I'll be setting foot in uncharted territory, not because I'm uncertain about where I'm heading. "Of course I know what day it is, Mama."

"Have you given the subject of readiness any more thought?" It's a rare day off for my mother, and I've done what I can to enhance it. When I woke up this morning, I went down to the Global Village Coffee Shop and picked up two chai lattes and a freshly baked loaf of organic banana bread, which we're now sharing. Her tired feet are propped up on pillows at the end of the couch. I have a feeling she's gonna stay in her pajamas all day, and I'm glad.

"I'm ready to start HRT. I've *been* ready…." I've been ready since I learned that taking cross-sex hormones was an option.

"The physical changes that estrogen brings about are irreversible. It's much different than the puberty blockers you're on now."

I realize it's my mother's obligation to remind me of this stuff. Just like it's my responsibility to discuss it with some semblance of maturity. After all, I'm making an adult decision. "Mama, Dr. Evelyn has given her recommendation to proceed, and I'm almost seventeen. It's better if I start now, rather than wait. Plus, it's what I want—I want to live in the right body. I need to…. It's time."

"Well, you know your… *your sperm*, Jules. It might not be viable if you—" It's got to suck for Mama to talk *sperm* with her only child, but she does it.

"I *need* to do this so I can *survive*." The volume of my voice increases as I'm on the path to losing my cool. But my *sperm* means nothing if *I'm* not here, right? "I can't go on like this! And I *understand*—Dr. Evelyn and you and the doctors have gone over the potential risks with me—but I have to become who I am. 'Cause I need to see *her* when I catch sight of my reflection in a window, and I need to feel like *her* on the inside even more, and the hormones will help make that stuff happen." I stand up in my spot on the floor beside the coffee table and glower down. I'm frustrated too, because I promised myself I wouldn't have this kind of shrieking spaz-out each and every time Mama tries to discuss the impact of taking hormones for the long term, and I failed once again. "I *know* about the freaking risk for heart disease and diabetes and blood clots—but do you know how it feels to be growing chest hair when all you want is boobs? *Do you?*"

Thankfully, Mama doesn't get pissed off that I lost it. "There's just so much they don't know medically about what you'll be doing—about cancer and…. Is 'passing' as a cisgender woman really *all that important*? Important enough to risk your health?"

I slip a heavy dose of acid into the look I send her. How can she equate my need to live my life in the right body to the desire to "pass" as a cisgender woman?

"Just listen to me, Jules, because there's something else I want you to consider. You are the single greatest love of my life… and you will most likely not be able to have children of your own. That is, unless we bank some of your sperm, like we discussed."

My mother is rambling on and on about all of her fears, and I guess it's her right, if not her responsibility. But I have rights too. "There are other ways to create a family—to have children *of my own*, even if they're not genetically related to me. Adoption is an option I think I'd really be into. And I plan to monitor my health carefully, *forever*, Mama, but I don't want to live as a boy—as a boy developing into a man—any longer. I can't…. Don't you get it?" I drop down beside her on the edge of the couch. "I'll never blame you for letting me do this. Because doing this... transitioning... it's my only chance." I don't mean to play the suicide card with my mother, but it is how I see transitioning at this point in my life. I can only go on as a girl, and then as a woman, and I will do everything I can to transition as fully as possible. "I need to try this."

The way she looks at me—with such compassion and confusion and hopefulness and fear—tells me why she needs to bring this topic up again and again. There will be no surprises when it comes to my choice to make this change; there will be no occasion for me to say to her, "Mama, I didn't know! Nobody told me *this* would happen!"

Despite the torturous worry that her love for me invites, Mama needs to accept that I *must* take the risks that come with the miracle of transitioning. Even if I'm not sure exactly how far I'll go on my journey to become physically the person I already know I am inside.

Will my body be able to tolerate taking hormones? And will I choose to undergo surgeries in my effort to transition? Or will I come to a place where I feel I'm a woman, regardless of body characteristics that suggest otherwise? Will I eventually decide that my gender is strictly in my own head and, like Mama said, "passing" isn't all that important?

I don't yet know all of the answers, and I don't have to know. I just need to do whatever it takes to let me live in reality right now.

"It'll be all right. It'll be fine. You'll see." I lift her cup of chai from the table and place it in her hand. "Now, you need caffeine, Mama, and badly. So drink this."

She smiles and takes a sip.

We sit there in chai-latte-sipping silence until I get a text message from Kale.

Kale: *Can you and the girls come with me again to look for Hughie?*

Julian: *No prob. Come get me—I'll wait for you at the Global Village. Then we can pick up the girls together.*

Kale: *Great. Thanks.*

Julian: *Since we're going to look for Hughie, I assume you haven't heard from him yet. How are you holding up?*

Kale: *Been better. But I'll survive. How does an hour sound?*

Julian: *Sounds good. Later....*

"Who was that, Julian?"

"This kid named Kale. He's kind of a new friend—I met him at the town human rights group I joined, but he also goes to my school."

"Does he know what you are going through right now?"

I'm almost certain she means my transition. "He's not that close of a friend yet."

"Is he your boyfriend?"

"No!" Shit. *Nothing* is sacred with Mama.

"Would you like him to be?"

I decide not to honor her last question with an answer, mainly because I don't know the answer. "His cousin ran away from home. And as it turns out, I know the kid—Hugh Oswald."

"He's that very bright boy who's in all your classes, right? I think you've mentioned him."

"Yeah, Hughie's a brain. I'm gonna go help Kale find him. We have a few ideas of places to look."

"Nowhere dangerous, I hope."

Yet another question that really can't be answered. "I won't be late."

"Well, give your mama a nice hug, and if I'm sleeping when you come in, wake me up to let me know you're home."

I lean over and hug her, and I know that even though our conversation wasn't easy, everything is okay between us. Mama's got my back.

Kale, 1:00 p.m.

I SHOULDN'T be noticing Julian the way I'm noticing him today. I mean, my cousin is out on the street, mostly because I have zero compassion, and I'm ogling a member of the rescue party.

I will say Julian gawked at me for a few seconds when he climbed into the minivan because I'm wearing a baseball cap. When I first got dreads, I stopped wearing baseball caps, as they crushed the mushroom, so to speak. But today I'm in my mother's *Bad Hair Day*

103

ball cap that she wears on early mornings when she hits the gym. She says it saves her long explanations with regard to why her hair isn't styled to its usual impeccable standard.

My mind strays back to the gay thing.

I hadn't given the possibility of being gay any serious consideration at all, like, in my entire life, until I met Julian and became obsessed with his lips. Maybe there was no room for "am I gay?" anxiety because I was so preoccupied with the whole "am I a hippie?" thing. But right now, I find myself stealing quick peeks at the soft, wavy hair that falls over Julian's shoulders. And wanting to stick my nose into it.

First it was his lips, and then it was his eyes. Now I'm caught up in his hair. Soon I'll be drooling over his nose, or his chin, maybe—this can't be normal! He's a *guy*. And weirder still, the stuff I like about him most is the least masculine stuff. Mine is a twisted way of being gay; that's all I know. I clearly need to conduct extensive online research on this topic, but that can't happen today.

"That's Anna's house. The yellow ranch on the right." I tear my eyes from his hair and pull into the driveway that Julian points out. "Kandy ended up sleeping over here last night, so we don't have to trek over to her house to pick her up."

"Cool." Is it cool? Or is *cool* some trendy word I started saying when I thought I was a hippie? My brief career as a free-spirited hippie came to its speedy conclusion last night when I lost the dreads. And the cool dude attitude.

"Anna! Kandy! I bought you mocha lattes with extra whipped cream at the Global Village—they're in the back-seat drink holders."

Julian had arrived at the minivan today carrying a drink holder filled with four specialty coffees. It was thoughtful, especially since I'm pretty sure his funds are low.

"Hey, boys!" Anna gets in the back seat and Kandy runs around the other side to hop in behind me. "Any word from Hughie?"

I shake my head.

"So what's the plan? Where are we going to look for him?" I'm getting used to Kandy's waste-no-time attitude. I think I like it too.

But everybody looks to me because this *is* my ball game. "I thought we'd check the mall again and the movie theater, and maybe a few of the rest areas on the highway. I don't know of any crack houses to check out, do you guys?"

My three passengers look at each other and shake their heads. Anna blushes.

"I think we should start at the rest area near exit 23, though, since we didn't look there yesterday."

"Sure thing."

As I drive, the girls discuss our possible approach, in the event we actually come across Hughie at the rest area. They are incredibly tuned in to what Hughie might be feeling in ways that never crossed my mind.

"He'll probably be asking himself why he should come with us. I mean, he took off for a reason, and as far as he knows, nothing has changed," Kandy says over the sound of the downtown traffic.

She's right. As far as *I* know, nothing *has* changed.

"So, he'll be scared and confused. What will you say to him, Kale? How will you calm him down and let him know that things will be okay if he decides to come with us?" Anna asks.

That's a very good question. "I... well, I'm not too sure...."

Julian glances at me from the passenger street and says, "I wouldn't get in this van if I were him, not unless I knew for a fact I wasn't gonna get sent to live in a place where I don't feel safe."

All I can do is nod.

"So what *is* your plan, Kale? You need a plan." I'm starting to expect comments like this from Kandy.

"I guess I'll just say that my dad loves him and I'm pretty sure he'll fight to keep him at our house."

Anna replies quickly. "It wouldn't hurt to remind him that you and your mother care too."

Again, I nod. She's right, assuming Mom actually cares about anything other than the next buy-one-get-one-free sale.

"It's time to step up to the plate, Kale." Julian is looking out the window, suddenly deep in thought. Without glancing my way, he asks me quietly, "But *can* you step up to the plate?"

105

"Like am I *capable*?"

"Yeah... are you?"

I look at him across the center console. I feel like his reasons for asking me this run far deeper than just the Hughie situation. "I... I think so."

It's quiet in the van until I pull onto the highway.

Anna breaks the silence. "This mocha is delicious, Julian."

"It really is. Thank you, hon."

These girls are great. And I don't miss that in my time of need I didn't call Robbie and Jared, the kids I hang around with at lunch and on the rare weekend nights I go out. I called Julian and his two BFFs. Maybe I should take a page from their playbook and say thank you. "I never had a mocha latte before. It was really good. So... thanks."

Even if it wasn't made with almond milk.

Or maybe *because* it wasn't made with almond milk.

Julian, 5:00 p.m.

HUGHIE WASN'T at the rest area, the mall, the movie theater, any of the nearby diners or fast-food restaurants. Wherever he is, he doesn't want to be found.

Back in the minivan, driving rather aimlessly, Kale answers a call from his father. "Yeah, Dad, I get it. Tomorrow morning you're going to report him to the police as missing.... No, I don't think you're being irresponsible by waiting to file the report. We know he ran away... and we're both looking for him. Mom asked the ladies at the thrift shop to keep an eye out for him? Wow. I guess she's worried too. Okay... I'll be back before it's too late.... Yeah, you too. Bye."

Now that we've dropped the girls off, Kale and I are alone in the van. I can ask him anything since it's just the two of us. "That was your father?"

"Yeah. And he's frantic, for the most part."

"It sounds like he's more than just Hughie's uncle."

"He really loves Hughie—they have a lot in common. They're meat connoisseurs of the highest caliber."

I smile because that's kind of cute. "So what now?"

Kale pulls over in a vacant lot beside the old movie theater. "I can't think of anywhere else to look. He's always gone to the same places."

"Didn't you say he went to live under the Filmore Bridge when he had nowhere else to go?"

Kale nods. "Yeah, but my father told me that it's all fenced off so the homeless kids can't get under there anymore."

"Well, let me clue you in: a fence wouldn't stop me from getting under that bridge if it's where I wanted to be."

He looks at me, surprised. No, he's shocked. Being an apparently strict rule-follower, I doubt that Kale has ever even considered disobeying a Do Not Enter sign. I, however, am the polar opposite of a person who gets in line behind everybody else to do the "right" thing. I mean, I won't even accept the gender I was assigned at birth.

Kale pulls off his baseball cap to rub his forehead as this unconventional concept sinks into his mind.

"What it says on that cap is like the understatement of the year." He looks at me again when I say this, but now he's just curious. "You *are* having a bad hair day."

He runs his fingers through his short, uneven blond spikes. "Yeah… about my hair…."

"I thought you were a hippie, *dude*." I can't cut the sarcasm from my tone.

"I thought I was too." Kale puts the minivan in drive and then says in an uneasy tone I haven't heard before, "I was wrong."

Kale, 6:00 p.m.

JULIAN WAS right. The fence surrounding the base of the Filmore Bridge is bent in some places and completely knocked down in others. A length of wire-mesh didn't stand a chance against the iron will of desperate teenagers.

It's getting dark and is already pretty cold. The wind is picking up; soon it'll be frigid. I hope my brosin isn't out here. Nobody should be out here.

Julian ran out ahead of me and is stomping on a length of fence that's sagging toward the ground. "Come on! We can get in right here!"

I walk over to where Julian is pounding the fence into the ground with his combat boots. "I think I see some light over there, by the edge of the bridge."

He looks in the direction that I'm pointing. "Yeah, I think there are some people there. We have to be quiet—we don't want to spook them."

I step up beside him on top of the wire fencing that's now flat on the ground. "If he's here... if he's here, I don't have a clue what I'm g-going to s-say to him." My voice is shaky and I'm not sure why. This my *Hughie* I'm talking about. Piece-of-furniture-in-my-bedroom Hughie!

Flicking on his phone's flashlight, Julian leads the way. "Just tell him the truth. You know, tell him how you feel."

I've never been big on spilling my guts. "Right... I-I can do that."

"I'm serious. Honesty—best policy, you know?"

I swallow back my worry and follow him over a pile of sticks and leaves, and then across a dirt lot. From our spot behind a row of scraggly trees, we can see an orange and green tent, a small campfire, and about six teenagers standing around it.

"Hey—who's over there?" one of them yells.

"We can hear you! And we can see your flashlight!"

"What if it's the cops?"

"They woulda busted us already."

Julian steps out of the trees, and I see no choice but to follow him. He shouts, "It's just us—just a couple of kids like you! We're looking for my friend's cousin, Hughie Oswald."

No sooner has Julian finished speaking than we see somebody scramble out of the tent and take off in the direction of the bridge.

"That's Hughie!" I'm after him in a split second.

The teens standing by the fire start shouting again. "Hey, leave Oswald alone—he didn't do nothin' to you!"

"He doesn't have to go with you assholes!"

Julian stays behind to settle the crowd while I chase Hughie under the bridge. I'm bigger than him and faster too, and it takes me less than thirty seconds to catch up with him. I grab him by the sweatshirt and we both tumble to the ground. "Hughie, calm down! I'm here to help you!"

"Let me go! You better let me go!" Underneath me, Hughie starts to twist and turn, and when he gets a little freedom, he takes a few swings that miss by a mile. "I'm not going back to her!"

It takes a few more seconds to pin him down. And when I do, my brosin is close to crying. "You don't have to go back to Mary Pat! So just chill out!"

Although it's getting dark, I can see his face clearly. He has a black eye, a swollen lip, and dirt on his face. But I see zero trust there. "Why'd you come here, then?" he sneers. "You never cared before if I lived or died!"

Ouch. The truth hurts. Still gripping him tightly with my fists, I reply, "I came to find you and to bring you back to our house. Shit, Hughie. I came to take you home—to *your* home."

He shakes his head. "You wouldn't do that for me." Hughie struggles a bit more, but not as fiercely as before.

Double ouch. "You're wrong." I get why he'd see it that way. And maybe a few days ago, I would have agreed. But today I know he's wrong.

"If you bring me back, I'm just gonna bolt again...."

His eyes are glassy, not that he's looking at me, and it doesn't surprise me at all when tears trickle down both sides of his face. "Hughie—if you run away again, then I'll have to come find you again."

This is when Hughie lets go and starts bawling. "Just leave me here, Crunchy. Pretend you never saw me. *Please*...."

He isn't struggling anymore, so I loosen my grip on his sweatshirt. I flop down on top of him, exhausted from the chase and all the emotions. "Dad's losing it—he's so worried about you. He won't make you go back to live with your mother. I promise."

After a little bit more sniffing and snorting, Hughie replies in a weak voice, "How do you know? Uncle Sam is nuts about his little sister, 'Serenity.'"

"Listen to me carefully." I lift myself off him so I can see his face.

Hughie still won't look me in the eyes. "To what?"

"To the truth… that Dad's pretty crazy about *you* too." I flop back down on his belly.

The strangest thing happens. I feel hands grasping my jacket, as tightly as I had a hold of Hughie's sweatshirt. He's pulling me toward him…. *Hughie's hugging me.*

I lower my voice and make my confession. "I've been a pretty shitty cousin, and I know it."

"Nah, you let me share your room… and your dad."

"It'll be better when you come back. Maybe we can be more like… brothers." Strangely, I really mean this. I don't know why it took me so long to realize that being brothers would be better than being cousins, or even brosins.

Hughie's sobbing has stopped; now he's just breathing heavy. And he doesn't challenge me on the *brothers* thing. He just lies there, so I sink against him.

Soft footsteps come up behind us. "Hey." It's Julian.

I drag my body off Hughie's and then pull him to his feet. Hughie keeps his head low, refusing to make eye contact with either of us.

"I aced our FDR presentation yesterday," Julian offers.

Hughie blinks.

"There's gonna be another project, due right before vacation." Julian takes a step closer to Hughie. "I was counting on you being my partner again. Nobody else in that class is worthy."

All Hughie does is shrug.

"I'm gonna take *that* as a superenthusiastic yes."

"Let's go home, Hughie." I step up beside him, and I want to wrap my arm around his shoulder so much, but can't bring myself to do it. Instead I pat his forearm.

Baby steps, I think.

"I don't have a home," he replies.

"Yeah, you do. And I have a feeling that you're in for a double-meatfest tonight. Nobody ate last night's Mexican Meat Fiesta. Dad'll probably heat that up *and* do his regular Winter Chill Grill."

This makes Hughie smile. "I'm pretty hungry."

The three of us walk back toward the group of teens and the tent. "You took your backpack with you when you left, right? Is it in the tent?"

Hughie nods. "It's in the tent. I'll grab it. And I want to say goodbye to the others."

"Of course."

Hughie leaves to go grab his stuff in the tent. Julian has been quiet up until now, but he asks, "Is he okay? It looks like he got beat up."

"I didn't ask him about it. I figure once we get him into the van, we can ask whatever we want. He'll be trapped."

Julian snickers. "You're evil."

"An evil genius, maybe." I look over to the small crowd standing by the fire. "Do you recognize any of those kids, from school or anything?"

Julian is quiet for a few seconds, and then he replies, "I recognize myself in one of them."

I find this a very strange response, but before I have a chance to ask him about it, Hughie climbs out of the tent. "I'm ready to go home."

He throws the backpack, which appears to be stuffed full of textbooks, over his shoulder and heads in the direction we came from. As we walk past the campfire, my attention is caught by a wild peal of laughter. I glance over at the group of teenagers, curious to see the homeless guy who's happy enough to laugh with such abandon, and what I see causes me to stare. Because I don't see a guy at all.

I'm not really sure how to categorize the person who is bent over in laughter. Because the person is definitely trying to look like a *he*—buzzed hair and a thick leather jacket and sagging jeans and work boots—but I can tell that the body beneath the clothes is a girl's.

"He was kicked out of his house. Because of how he is." Julian stops walking in order to inform me of this. "He told me so." He watches me closely.

He. Julian called the person who is clearly a girl dressed like a boy, *he.* I stop beside him and look back at the teen by the campfire, who's now saying goodbye to Hughie. All I can think of to say is, "That sucks."

"Yeah, it sure as hell does," Julian says and continues to study me.

I feel uncomfortable, so I tell them, "Come on, you guys. We need to get home before Dad loses it."

Julian, 9:00 p.m.

YOU COULD say that Sam Oswald is extremely happy to have Hughie back home, if happy is defined as: relieved to the point of hyperventilation combined with ecstatic to the point of weepiness. After hugging Hughie and then Kale and then Hughie and then me and then Hughie again, and doing this little ritual no less than ten times over, he finally puts the Mexican Meat Fiesta in the microwave for our "hearty appetizer" and gets the grill going for the "protein-packed main course."

Since Kale is a vegetarian, he doesn't eat, as he calls them, "the goodies from the barnyard," but he downs half a jar of Skippy Crunchy Peanut Butter on hamburger buns. And too many baby carrots to count.

Now, as we sit around the kitchen table, I'm welcomed into an intimate family moment, where Hughie, Kale, and Mr. Oswald discuss plans to make Hughie's living situation at the Oswald home permanent. Apparently, Mrs. Oswald couldn't be here as she's at a Designer Pocketbook Party at the next-door neighbor's house, but she left a box of bakery cupcakes on the kitchen island. I think Kale was disappointed that his mom wasn't here to greet Hughie, but he never actually said so.

"I'm sorry I didn't tell your mother that she hadn't acted like a proper guardian for you in many years, Hugh. And it's not because she's an adult entertainer that her mothering is inadequate. It's because

Mary Pat is reckless with you. For years, she's been out all hours of the night and left you alone, and I don't think it was right for her to bring home so many different male overnight guests." He clears his throat. "I regret not speaking up—you'll never know how much. I guess I was just trying to keep the peace in our family."

"What if Mary Pat sues you to get me back—you know, in a court with a lawyer and a judge?" Hughie has little faith in anybody.

"I won't let it come to that. I'm going to her apartment to discuss this situation with her tomorrow morning."

"What if she won't take no for an answer?"

"Hugh, I will stand behind you in any way necessary. Whatever it takes, this is your home from now on."

"Mary Pat is gonna want to see me…. I'm sure of it."

"Then she can come to see you here—with us—when you're ready to see her."

Every concern Hughie comes up with is squelched by Kale's dad, which is awesome. Mama would do that for me.

"But you need to promise that you won't run away again, son. My heart can't take it."

Hughie doesn't offer a promise, but he looks his uncle in the eye and smiles.

Kale says almost nothing over dinner. This could be because his mouth is stuck shut with all that peanut butter, or it could be that he has no idea what to say. But as we eat the cupcakes, Kale finally spills what's been on his mind. "Hughie's mother is not the only one with issues. Mom should be here right now—it's an important night."

Mr. Oswald nods. "You're right, son. All of us need to get our priorities in order. I'm going to see to it that this happens. Your mother might need to talk to a professional about her feelings over losing her job. You can be sure I'll discuss this with her." Mr. Oswald wipes his eyes with a paper towel and changes the subject. "Hughie, you look bushed. I think it's time you get to bed."

"I didn't sleep very well over the past couple of nights."

"It was damned cold outside, and it kills me to think of you sleeping in a tent." Mr. Oswald stands. "You could probably use a hot shower, and I want to take a look at your lip. I think it's infected."

Hughie gets up quickly, eager to sleep in his own bed.

"Glad you're back, Hughie. And thanks for dinner, Mr. Oswald."

"It was my pleasure, Julian. Thank you for helping to find Hughie—who is never going to go missing again. Right?" He winks at me and then again looks to Hughie, who has mastered the art of the poker face.

"I'm on dish duty," Kale says to his dad.

"I appreciate that, Kalin." Mr. Oswald smiles at him.

"Hughie, I'm glad you're back, too, you know."

"Thanks, Kale." Hughie shrugs and follows his uncle down the hall. "Kale's hair, Uncle Sam—major improvement, not that he asked me."

"I heard that…." Kale rubs his hands over his head like he forgot his dreadlocks were history.

"Dish duty won't be a problem, will it?" I look around the kitchen table at all of the paper plates and plastic cups and utensils.

"It never is. Basically dish duty means clearing off the table into the trash and putting away the ketchup, mustard, steak sauce, and bag of baby carrots."

Dinner at Kale's house, food-wise, was not a major improvement over dinner at mine, but it had a nice family flair. "Let me give you a hand." I get up and start collecting the plastic cups. "You guys recycle?"

Kale's face turns red. "I tried to get our family to do better in the recycling department when I was… you know, when I was obsessing over keeping the earth green. But I gave up. Dad's a one-industrial-sized-garbage-bag-a-day kind of guy." He frowns. "I'm going to talk to him about this again when things settle down with Hughie."

It only takes five minutes to clean up. "I guess I should head home. My mother will be getting worried soon."

"You trust me to drive you home, or are you going to insist on taking the bus again?"

He has no idea that until I felt I knew him well enough, I literally *couldn't* get into a vehicle with him. For people like me who don't fit into the traditional gender boxes, driving off alone in the night with a relative stranger can feel very dangerous. But I know Kale well enough now to feel safe—I've been alone with him plenty of times. "I'm cool with a ride home."

We grab our coats and head for the door, but before Kale opens it, he looks right at me and says, "Thanks a lot. You helped me so much over the past couple of days."

Even though the hallway is dark, I see a look in his eyes that tells me he really means it. And that he's a little bit surprised by this.

Chapter 14—Sunday

Julian, noon

I SLEEP in because I know I won't have another chance until February vacation starts, which is over a week from now. I'm ashamed to admit, even to myself, that it's almost noon and I'm still lazing the day away in bed.

Next Saturday we have to get up early to drive to Norwell because the results of my blood tests will be in, and if everything looks good, I'll get my prescription for estrogen. Like Mama said, it's a big day, and one I've been waiting for since before I knew I was waiting, because I've been a girl inside for as long as I can remember, even if I don't live as one. I was a girl when I was five and I wished that the Tonka dump truck I got for Christmas was a Bratz Doll; I was a girl when I was seven and I snuck into my mother's bedroom to try on her shoes before I put on my cleats for Little League tryouts; I was a girl on Halloween when I was nine and I stood in front of the full-length mirror on my bedroom door and pretended I was the Little Mermaid when I was dressed up as Bob the Builder.

I'm a girl right now as I lie in my bed and think about what happened over the past few days. And what's going to happen over the next few weeks.

Maybe helping to find Hughie made me consider stuff that hadn't occurred to me before. I don't think I'm the only one who has it hard in my high school anymore. And I can't imagine what it would be like to have a mother who didn't support me. When I was at my lowest point, Mama lifted me back up. How messed-up would it be if my mother was *the reason* I hit rock bottom, like Hughie's mom?

116

If I lie in bed any longer, I'm going to lose my freaking mind with this overthinking, though. I should get up. I lean over and grab my phone off the bureau beside the bed.

Julian: *Anna, Kandy: Good news. We found Hughie!*

Anna: *OMG. That's great!*

Kandy: *Where on earth was he? We looked everywhere....*

Julian: *Not everywhere. We didn't look under the bridge—at least, not until last night after we dropped you guys off.*

Kandy: *I thought it was blocked off.*

Julian: *Not blocked off well enough to stop Hughie and a bunch of other kids from setting up a tent and a campfire and calling it home.*

Anna: *It's hard to imagine there being homeless kids living right in Crestdale.*

Kandy: *It really is—those poor kids.*

Anna: *Let's go down there next week with some sandwiches and water... and blankets.*

Kandy: *Good thinking. So, is Hughie back at home now?*

Julian: *Yup. Safe and sound.*

Kandy: *You gonna keep hanging out with Kale now that his cousin's back home?*

Julian: *Good question.*

Anna: *Shoot. I have to go now—time to babysit.*

Kandy: *For the twins? You're so lucky! They're adorable.*

Anna: *Not when they're both crying. LOL. Catch you guys later.*

Julian: *I should go too. Homework calls. I'm a day behind.*

Kandy: *Looks like I'm going shopping alone. Later, guys!*

After showering, I go downstairs to the kitchen where I tidy up. As I empty the dishwasher, I am nearly knocked over by a predictable case of the guilts. Mama is long gone. She left for work when I was still out cold. I hope like hell the insurance company considers the letter from the Gender Center—it's our only chance.

Part of me wants to tell Mama that this whole transitioning thing can wait so she can stop working all of these exhausting extra hours. I wish I could tell her that my gender dysphoria isn't killing me and I can deal with it, but a bigger part of me knows that it might. Kill me, that is. I have to go forward with this.

On a sudden impulse, I run up the stairs and down the short hall and into my room, and within a few seconds I'm ripping through the junk on top of my desk. Then I tear into my deep bureau drawers in search of my Transition Journal, the diary that Dr. Evelyn strongly suggested I write in to keep track of my changing emotions as my body and mind undergo the journey from Julian to Julia. Finally, I find it under my bed, pressed against the wall where I stuck it in a moment of frustration. This journal was a "no-occasion gift" from Mama—but I think there was an occasion, after all.

And the big event was that I didn't die.

I dust off the bright red cover and run my fingers over the words *Dream, Hope, Live* that are embossed into the leather. I flip through the empty pages; they are the blank slate that *I'm not,* because the transition to Julia has already begun. It started before I can even remember, maybe even on the day I was born into the wrong body. No wonder I had no clue how to start this journal.

Most of Julian is already Julia.

I pull out the chair and push aside the mess on the desk so there's room for my journal. I open it to the first page, and without entering a date, I fill the blank page with words:

It happened today. This morning in my kitchen. To be exact, it hit me as I emptied the dishwasher and was stacking the spoons in their correct slot in the silverware drawer. They fell into place effortlessly because they were all spoons. Everybody knows a spoon wouldn't fit so well in the fork pile, which is what I'm trying to do by living as a boy when I'm a girl. It's time I join the other spoons.

I'm sure it's not this simple for all people who live with gender dysphoria, and it doesn't have to be. But this is my journey, and for me, it's plain and simple: I feel like a spoon in a pile of forks.

What I have to do is make a resolution, because without broad declarations to myself I'd still be 100% Julian, trying and failing at being a boy who is growing into a man.

So here it is: On the day I start taking hormones I will also start presenting as Julia. I will officially change from a "he" to a "she" in every way.

It's not gonna be easy. I'm definitely going to have to leave Crestdale High to attend the online secondary school that Mama and me decided on, because I'm not up to dealing with the crap that'll be dished out at Crestdale HS if I show up in a dress, as a girl named Julia who used to be Julian. It just won't fly.

So next Saturday I'll start estrogen, and the other drugs the endocrinologist prescribes to begin my transition.

Over February vacation, I'll start to adjust to the hormones, and once vacation is over I will attend school in front of a computer in my living room.

I'll live as Julia because I am Julia.

None of it will be easier to do in March or April. So I'll do this at the end of February.

I FINALLY started writing in my Transition Journal; Dr. Evelyn's gonna be thrilled.

I wonder how my new friend Kale will feel about my absence at school.

CHAPTER 15—WEDNESDAY

Kale, 4:00 p.m.

I ATE a grilled cheese sandwich on white bread and smiley-shaped french fries in the school cafeteria. White bread, that's what I said. There was nothing crunchy about it. And it was the bright orange American cheese, not goat cheese or creamy tofu cheese that was fried between those slices of bleached white bread. I'm also nearly 100 percent certain that the potatoes from which the smiley fries were cut were not organic. But I ate this lunch, with a side of completely un-crunchy black raspberry Jell-O that I know is not vegetarian, and I liked it and I would do it again.

I have not spoken the word "dude" aloud for three and a half days.

My T-shirt is a stretchy poly/cotton blend, rather than a fabric made from locally grown hemp.

And right now, standing in front of the school building, waiting for Mom to pick me up, which she'll do as soon as her eyebrow threading appointment has come to its trendy conclusion, I'm listening to Vampire Weekend on my iPhone, which isn't hippie, but sure is hipster.

My hippie days are over. I'm not crunchy anymore.

Times change. People change. That's all.

CHAPTER 16—FRIDAY

Julian, 4:00 p.m.

"I THINK we're ready for tomorrow, Julian. And I feel very good about the progress we've made in counseling."

"So glad I have your blessing, Dr. E." Something about my therapist brings out the snarkiness in me. Maybe she provides me with a safe zone to release my frustration. But my attitude never seems to get under her skin, despite the effort I put into it. And what's with the *we* thing? *I'm* the one who's come clean about what it is to be a girl trapped in a boy's body.

As usual, Dr. Evelyn ignores my sarcasm. "Now, you haven't told me much about the human rights group at the Community House that you've been taking part in. Are you still involved in it?"

"I'm running it now." I keep a straight face. It isn't easy.

Dr. Evelyn giggles. "I'll just bet you are."

"Actually, REHO is going pretty well. I got *way* into doing a project to help an elderly woman. And I met a kid who's become a friend—but don't get too excited about it."

"Why not? Making a new friend is exciting."

"He's one of those rule-follower types. And I'm kind of busy breaking the rules, aren't I?"

"How do you mean, 'breaking the rules,' Julian?"

"You're a smart lady. I don't have to spell it out for you, Dr. Evelyn. But I *will* suggest that I'm not exactly following *the gender rules*."

Dr. Evelyn shakes her head and her ponytail bounces back and forth over her shoulders. It's cute and perky and feminine. I want to wear my hair in a ponytail like that too. In public. "If he's your friend,

121

he'll stick by you because he'll realize that male or female, you are still you."

"Nice thought, Dr. E. I guess we'll see."

"Well, I hope it goes smoothly at your appointment at the Gender Center tomorrow, and by the time I see you next week, you'll be Julia, almost a week on hormones."

I get this prickly feeling all over my arms when she says that I'll be Julia next week. It's mostly a good prickly feeling.

If I had one wish, though—a wish aside from all things gender related—it would be that Kale would somehow understand this.

I like Kale. Maybe I like him a little bit too much, in a way he wouldn't appreciate. I think maybe he likes me a little too, but will he like Julia?

Because she is who I am.

Kale, 8:10 p.m.

I'M REALLY looking forward to seeing Julian at REHO tonight. Not that I haven't caught a few glimpses of him this week. I saw him in passing a few times in the cafeteria at lunchtime. I guess I could have invited him to eat lunch at my table. And the truth is I really wanted to, but Robbie and Jared just aren't cool enough to *get* Julian. Not like I do.

As usual, my eyes are glued to the stairs as I wait impatiently for Julian's arrival. I should have called him to see if he needed a ride here tonight so he didn't have to take the city bus. *Why didn't I do that?* Maybe because it might have seemed too much like a date... or maybe because I was freaked out that I *wanted* it to be a date. I'll make up for it by driving him home tonight.

And like a prince, he comes down the stairs with his head held high, giving the expression "better late than never" a stylish new meaning. It's impossible for me to do anything but stare, so that's what I do.

Judy must have a sixth sense about when Julian is going to arrive because she doesn't call the group to the circle until he's on the bottom step. "Okay, people, it is time for the meeting to begin. Let's form a circle and recite the pledge."

Julian walks right to my side and takes my hand, even before the others have joined the circle. I like the way his smaller hand feels in mine. I like looking down into his smart dark eyes. I like the way his hair is tied into a high bouncy ponytail. I like his silky button-down shirt and his genie pants and I especially like his blue suede shoes, which sounds clichéd, but he's really wearing them. Add these things to how much I like his lips and his eyes and his chin… I come to a sudden conclusion.

I have it bad for Julian Mendez.

The circle around me fills in with people, but honestly, I hardly notice, because I'm caught up in this moment.

Is this crush I have on the big personality or the boy himself?

I really don't know the answer, but I do know it feels like, since I met Julian, everything has changed in my life.

"We gather tonight in the spirit of love and selflessness, and with the solemn hope that our efforts to serve the community will be sufficient to keep hope alive for those who struggle to obtain the rights inherent to all human beings."

With no squeeze to pass around the circle, we all look to Judy to start the meeting.

"I'd like to begin tonight with some wonderful news," she says, wearing a smile I think I'd call smug.

I look around the circle and see the familiar faces of Paulina and Billy and Karima and Tom. Edna, it seems, has invited Tom's aunt, Tilly, to REHO. She winks at me when our gazes meet, since she's holding Edna's and Billy's hands and can't wave. Already this group has started to feel like a family to me. It happened so fast. Weird.

"Thanks to the effort of the Crosswalk Timers Group, an official complaint will be addressed at the next town meeting, requesting that the amount of time to cross Bay Road in front of the Beautiful Sunset Senior Center increase from twenty to thirty seconds in the interest of safety for the elderly and other people who need additional time."

The group breaks into noisy applause, and then almost everybody rushes toward Edna to hug her and congratulate her on the victory. I let go of Julian's hand, even though I don't really want to. "Nice going, Julian. Your work made a difference."

"It was a group effort," he reminds me, but we both know he was the guy behind the big idea.

After our impromptu victory celebration, it's time to get the pillows and spread them on the floor. I fetch my own, as well as Julian's purple one, and place them side by side. They say twice is a habit, don't they? Whoever the heck *they* are.

"Tonight I thought we'd talk about future goals for the group. Since it went so well when we focused on a group member's specific needs, I thought I'd ask if any other member has a personal-human-rights need that we could help with." Judy looks so pleased it makes me smile.

Tilly is the first to reply. "The issue I'd like to take a look at is body image. I'm a part-time pianist at a ballet school, and I often hear the young girls, and even the boys, talking about their fear of gaining weight. Some of them admit to one another that they starve themselves. One teen might say to another, 'I haven't had a bite to eat all day' at a 6:00 p.m. class." She stops talking to shake her head. "They think they won't get into the most select summer intensives if they aren't stick figures. And the sad fact is, I don't think this feeling is prominent only at ballet schools. I think this is a cultural problem that interferes with quality of life for more people than we realize."

As a group we brainstorm some ways we could encourage body positivity at Tilly's ballet school. After that, we talk about a possible adopt-a-grandchild program that Billy and Edna would like REHO to facilitate. And when it's time for the meeting to end, Julian stands. "Before we leave, I'd like to mention something that's important to me."

All eyes are glued to Julian as he steps to the front of the room.

"The members of this group have promised to support the rights of the elderly, people of different races and religions and sexualities, people who look ways that might be called unusual, and people with all kinds of other challenges. It means a lot—it means a lot *to me…*

124

and to all of us. I guess it's why we're here." He takes a deep breath, looks down at his blue suede shoes, and finishes. "*Everybody* has the right to be whoever he or she truly is without experiencing fear or pressure, and if we're *real* human rights advocates we won't forget this." He then nods once and steps back to his pillow.

Julian had been looking directly at me as he delivered the last sentence of his motivational reminder of why we all belong to REHO. It really should piss me off, because *duh—of course that's why we're all here,* but instead I feel guilty. And I know instantly that when we go back to school after vacation it'll be time for me to invite Julian to sit with my friends and me at lunch. Past time, probably. Oh, okay, it's *definitely* way past time I made this move, but I can't do anything about yesterday's bad behavior.

I promise myself I'm going to make more of an effort to be his friend, and not just at lunch in the caf, but in general. Jared and Robbie will have to deal with it. And doing this is no sacrifice at all because I genuinely like hanging out with Julian. Maybe I'll even get Julian and Anna and Kandy and Hughie together to see a movie over vacation.

After we put the pillows away, I approach Julian. "Would you like a ride home tonight?"

"It's out of your way. I'm fine with taking the bus."

"Well, I'm going to the Global Village Coffee Shop—I have a craving for another one of those mocha lattes—so your apartment isn't out of my way at all."

"I guess I'll hitch a ride with you, then."

He looks at me with those eyes, and a smile forms on those lips, and I hear myself ask, "Have a cup of coffee with me tonight, Julian?"

"I suppose I could do that." Julian stares at my face for a second before he looks away and pulls on his classy black trench coat.

Julian, 10:45 p.m.

"I LIKED what you said at the end of the meeting. It *was* dangerously close to a lecture, though." We sit across from each other in the same booth that we occupied last Thursday night when I was studying and Kale came here to see me, two nights before we found Hughie.

"If you think *that* was a lecture, you need to hear my mother when she gets going." I'm not throwing Mama under the bus. Just stating the truth. And there's a difference. "Anyway, how's Hughie doing?"

"I think he's glad to be home. And my father went and talked this situation out with his sister. He got her to agree to let Hughie stay with us until he graduates from high school and then on college breaks. Dad told me she sobbed, but he didn't let Hughie know that."

"That was probably a good idea. Did Hughie tell you where he was when he went missing?"

"Not really. He's not much of a talker. But I figure he was under the bridge for most of the time he was gone."

"Maybe you should ask him some questions about why he left and where he went. It wouldn't kill you." I stare him down easily. Kale clearly isn't proud of how he treated Hughie.

"I guess it *wouldn't kill me*. I'll talk to him about it." Kale looks back up at me. "Can I ask *you* some questions?"

I shiver and it's not cold in the café. "What do you want to know?"

"I want to know about what...." He sips his mocha and a tiny chocolate mustache clings to his top lip. "I want to know about why you... why you did what you did last fall." He wipes his wrist across his mouth and the mustache is gone.

"I did a lot of things last fall, Kale." Maybe playing dumb will get me out of this discussion.

"You know what I'm talking about."

"Maybe I do." I sniff. I know exactly what he's referring to—my attempt to prematurely meet my maker—but I *don't* know Kale well enough to arm him with my secrets. I don't trust him fully. "But why do you even care?"

Kale tilts his head. "I care about people." This claim comes out sounding like a question.

"Do you?"

"Well, I try to."

Is that good enough for me?

We look at each other through narrowed eyes.

And surprisingly, he lets me off the hook. "Okay, I get it. I pried into your private life. You don't have to tell me anything."

I swallow hard and nod. "Yeah, you *did* pry. So instead of telling you why I tried to check out of… of life, I'll tell you some things that were *not* the reasons I did it."

He tilts his head even farther. It's almost sideways now.

"I didn't try to… to do it… because I'm gay and I can't accept it."

"Okay."

"I didn't do it because I flunked out of math or because some teacher called home to tell my mother I have a smart mouth."

"You actually *do* have a very smart mouth."

"So I've been told. That wasn't why, though."

Kale is quiet, although his eyes bulge with questions. He wants to beg me to tell him my reasons for wanting to die, but he doesn't. I respect his restraint.

"All I'm gonna tell you is that I was feeling lost. And I don't expect you to understand it. I was just lost."

"Do you still feel lost?" Kale asks.

"Sometimes. But not like I did last fall."

"I feel lost sometimes too," he says, his eyes now glassy. I consider this to be a huge admission, and I can tell Kale does too. He looks away from me but keeps on talking. "I spent a lot of time trying to be someone I'm not."

Nobody could miss that Kale used to play the part of a hippie, but he hasn't acted like that since Hughie went missing.

He keeps talking before I have a chance to nod or comment. "And I haven't figured out exactly who I'm supposed to be." I had no idea Kale was capable of this kind of introspection, and the realization gives me hope. "Have *you*?"

I shake my head and then I nod. "I don't know. Maybe I'm getting there."

"Well, good. Then maybe there's hope for me too?" Kale's eyes are bright; he is also looking for reasons to hope. And I could confide

127

in him—I could tell him about my struggle and how my life is going to change, starting tomorrow.

But I don't. I just smirk. "I think there could be room for some limited hope."

The workers flash the overhead lights. I know they're signaling that it's time for us to clear out, as it's after eleven and the café is already closed. I start to get up, but I stop when Kale reaches across the table and grabs my hand. "I want to see you over vacation," he says quickly.

I look at our hands, entwined on the table. It's like there's energy running from my hand into his, and I wonder if this is what close friendship feels like or if it's something else. "I'm not gonna be around over vacation."

This is not a lie. Julian Mendez is not going to be around.... *Julia* Mendez is.

He looks disappointed. The light in his eyes dulls.

"But I'll be at REHO next Friday night. Will you be there?" I ask.

Kale nods eagerly. "Wouldn't miss it. Can I pick you up and drive you?"

"Uh… I don't think that would be such a good idea. I'll meet you there. 'Kay?"

"Sure… I guess." Momentarily Kale looks injured, but he rubs his nose with the back of his wrist and the hurt expression is gone. "Well, have a nice week." He lets go of my hand and stands up.

I look up at him. "It's going to be a very good week."

CHAPTER 17—FRIDAY

Kale, 6:30 p.m.

"HUGHIE, ARE you sure you don't want to come with me tonight? I think you'd like the Rights for Every Human Organization. And Julian said he'd be there—you like him, right?"

He's standing on his bed and hanging a poster of Albert Einstein on the wall because over vacation I told him it was time he added his personality to our bedroom decor.

"Yeah, I like Julian too, and thanks for the invite, but I'm kind of worn out from all the thumb wrestling we did, and Uncle Sam said he's gonna do a Winter Chill Grill. He wants to cook up a kielbasa storm since Aunt Kathy is out having a fanny facial at the Queen for a Day Spa downtown."

I decide not to ask for an explanation of *fanny facial,* as some knowledge cannot be unlearned. "Well, I'm going to shower and head over to the Community House."

"I'm gonna hang a Steve Jobs poster and then go rinse the baby carrots. Have a good time and say hi to Julian." Hughie is like a different guy since he's sure he's not going to be forced to relocate to Mary Pat's one-bedroom love nest.

As soon as I set foot in the shower, though, my mind throws a Julian Mendez-obsess-fest. It forgets to invite me but still, I listen in.

Why didn't Julian get back to me after I texted him today?

All I wanted was to see if he needed a ride to REHO tonight.

He shouldn't have to ride the dirty city bus when I'm happy to drive him.

Why didn't Julian text me back?

I step out of the shower and towel off the warm water on my skin and hair, which makes me think about hot yoga, effectively distracting me from worries over Julian. Over vacation, while Mom was at hot yoga, Hughie and I drank hot chocolate at the ice skating rink. When Mom got her hair extensions placed closer to her scalp, Hughie and I went to the Comic Book Crack House and got five issues of *The Unbeatable Squirrel Girl* to share. As Mom's armpit hair was removed by a laser, Hughie and I ate fast food. And then we challenged each other to a "loudest armpit fart contest." I won. And during her microdermabrasion appointment, well, Hughie and I just sat in the van and tried to figure out what the heck microdermabrasion is.

In other words, over February vacation, we bonded like we never had before.

I don't think Dad has talked to Mom about her priorities yet, but I promised him I'd be patient. And I think I get where she's coming from now. Mom lost something that meant a lot to her when she lost her job, and she's having trouble finding a new direction, and maybe even a new identity. I *so* get that.

I wrap the towel around my waist and head for my bedroom to get dressed.

Now it's time to face Julian Mendez after a week of thinking about him, and thinking about me, and thinking about him and me.

Kale, 8:10 p.m.

"WE GATHER tonight in the spirit of love and selflessness, and with the solemn hope that our efforts to serve the community will be sufficient to keep hope alive for those who struggle to obtain the rights inherent to all human beings."

He's not here.
Julian didn't come to REHO.
Maybe he forgot all about it.
Maybe he doesn't want to see me.

Maybe I should just get over him and get over myself, because I'm not even sure I'm gay. I should concentrate on doing what I'm supposed to be here to do: keeping hope alive for those who struggle to obtain the rights inherent to all human beings.

"Let's get our pillows, my dear friends, and be seated. I have a very special guest to introduce to you tonight. She would very much like to share her personal interest in Rights for Every Human Organization, as well as her story, with all of you," says Judy, speaking in a voice so quiet and smug that we're forced to be stone silent in order to hear her.

Our circle breaks apart and we head for the closet to pull out the throw pillows. Judy, I notice, grabs two pillows—the ratty couch cushion she usually goes for, and... and Julian's purple pillow.

I fight the urge to shout, "Hey! That's Julian's pillow and he's not here, so put it back!" But the pillows are the shared property of REHO—not one of them has anybody's specific name embroidered on the bottom—so I resist the urge and drop down obediently onto my pillow.

Judy lowers the lights, which makes me wonder *why the mystery?*— but again, I don't ask. Paulina glances over at me, as if to see if I know what's going on, but I shrug, and she looks away quickly.

"So who is this sp-sp-special guest, J-judy?" asks Tom. The suspense is getting to him too.

"You will see, soon enough."

Soon enough doesn't turn out to be very soon at all. We sit there in dim silence, for twenty minutes, at least, waiting for the sound of footsteps on the stairs. Finally, Judy's phone buzzes and she says, "Our guest has arrived."

For some reason we all continue to stare straight in front of us in the direction of the purple pillow at the front of the room rather than turning to gawk expectantly at the stairs. Finally, we hear a soft clicking of footsteps on the stairs. Footsteps that move slowly... reluctantly, even.

After a period of time that seems as interminable as winter vacation, a dainty and petite young woman, draped in a hooded cape— which I realize sounds cryptic, but also happens to be true—passes by us and makes her way to the front of the room. And she stands there.

"Let me help you with your coat, dear," Judy offers, but her determined tone suggests that she does not plan to take no for an answer.

The hooded head nods, and Judy draws the cape from her shoulders. Um... *his* shoulders.

The person standing in front of the room, gazing at some random spot above all of our heads, is Julian Mendez. *My* Julian, wearing a snug black dress and gray tights and boots that reach slender knees. *My* Julian, with maroon lips and lined eyes and hair that curls softly over feminine shoulders.

"I am pleased to introduce to you, *Julia* Mendez," Judy declares in the upbeat manner of a game show host.

My jaw drops. I feel like Hughie when I informed him that plants are people too.

"Please, everyone, say hello to Julia."

The entire REHO group, minus me, replies, "Hell-ooo, Ju-li-a." They do as they are told, but their eyes have grown every bit as wide as mine.

"Julia, do you have anything you'd like to say to the Rights for Every Human Organization?" Judy asks.

Without directly answering Judy's question, Julian/Julia takes a single step forward and speaks in a voice that's just a little bit softer and lighter than usual. "*Gender dysphoria* is what they call it. It sounds pretty straightforward—in a psycho-medical-babble way—but it isn't simple at all when it's real and is happening to you. So I thought I'd tell you what it's like. You know... how it feels."

I sit on my pillow and listen to Julian/Julia talk about how he made the decision to transition to female after his attempt to take his own life failed. And I hear his words, but I can't absorb them. I collect everything he says—commit it to memory—so I can obsess over it later, when I'm alone.

Julian/Julia swallows; it seems like telling this story is the hardest thing he's ever done. But I can't swallow. I can't breathe. I'm afraid I'm going to tip over—fall right off the edge of my pillow— and crash to the floor, making a total scene.

And Julian/Julia isn't finished. "In short, I have a conflict: my inner self doesn't match my outer self. But I *am* a girl—I'm a transgender girl. I'm Julia."

The REHO crowd is already murmuring things like, "you go, girl" and everyone is nodding, offering acceptance and support and applause.

I clap along with everyone else at the end of the "I'm Julia" speech. I clap because coming out and saying this to us was a brave thing to do. But my insides are screaming louder than the clapping.

My insides are screaming questions at *me*.

What does this make you, *Kale? Gay? Straight? Profoundly confused? What does the attraction you* still *feel for* this person *standing in front of the room mean* for you?

And so, as if this evening is all about me, I jump up, kick my pillow aside, stumble through the obstacle course of human rights advocates on low cushions and race up the stairs, and then I run recklessly along the yellow lines in the middle of the street, because I'm surely the only person on this street who is hurt and confused and angry. I let the traffic navigate its way around me, and I don't cross over to the sidewalk until I reach my mother's minivan.

CHAPTER 18—WEDNESDAY

Kale, noon

I HAVEN'T been stalking Julian/Julia. I wouldn't do something that creepy. But I just happened to notice that his profile has been entirely removed from Facebook. He definitely wasn't in the cafeteria Monday or Tuesday. And since I've just completed my third trip walking up and down the aisles between the lunch tables and studying each face, patrolling the nearby restrooms, and searching the alcove that encloses the food counters, I can reasonably conclude that he's not in the cafeteria today either.

With my hot lunch in hand—cheese pizza with a side of salad and cinnamon coffee cake for dessert—I sit down with Jared and Robbie.

"No pansy-ass granola bar for lunch today?" asks Robbie, as he shovels down his industrial-size salad. "I won't be able to call you Crunchy no more, and I'd sure miss that."

"*Pansy-ass* is a politically incorrect term. Call it a light snack, or maybe, an unsatisfying one," I counter.

"Aren't *we* sensitive today?" Robbie doesn't look up from his food, not even to dish out the harassment. "Shit, this salad is the balls."

"That salad could feed a family of five," Jared remarks. "I'll stick with my mother's cheddar and mango chutney cheese balls, thank you very much."

"Do either of you guys know Julian Mendez?" I blurt, only realizing it's a random question as it comes out of my mouth.

"Is he that homo-emo-brainiac? You know, the skinny kid who tried to off himself last fall?"

I shake my head at Robbie's callousness, but I don't correct him. "That'd be the kid."

134

Jared says, "He's in my precalc class. He pisses everybody off because his high scores throw off the bell curve—thanks to him our tests never get scaled."

"Has he been in class this week?" I ask, impatient for what I need to know.

Jared picks up a cheese ball and bites into it, causing mango chutney to explode from its center and onto his fingers. "Nope. Word is he quit school."

"He *what*?"

"Julian Mendez quit school. But, uh… what do you care?" Jared is onto me. I can tell by the way he lifts his eyebrows.

Before I have a chance to say that I *don't* care, but was just curious, Robbie informs us, "I saw him at the dollar store last night. That fag was wearing a dress… and looking at girls' clothes."

This statement catches Jared's attention. "You know, I heard that Mendez was turning into a girl. I thought it was nothing but gossip. Guess I was wrong." He licks his chutney-covered fingers.

"That's messed-up, if you ask me. But you never told us why you give a shit, Crunchy? What's the deal?" Robbie stops chewing.

I look at Jared, whose eyebrows are still raised, and then at Robbie, who has actually put his fork down as he waits to hear my reply. "*Jeez, you guys.* I don't give a crap about Julian Mendez, or if he's a dude or a lady. He's… he's just a friend of my cousin, Hughie. They're doing a project together, and Mendez has been among the missing. You know, so Hughie asked me if I had a clue where the kid was." A complete and total lie. "*Jeez.*"

Buying it, Robbie nods, picks up his fork, and shovels a clump of lettuce smothered in blue cheese dressing into his mouth. "Sucks for Hubie."

"Whatevs." Jared returns his focus to the gourmet cheese balls. "But that transgender shit is messed-up."

Transgender. Jared knows the word for what Julian/Julia says he is. And because of the fact that Julian/Julia is a transgender girl I have pulled a total Judas Iscariot on his ass. I've denied our friendship and anything else that had been growing between us.

Side note: Not that it makes a difference in my life, one way or the other, but last night I googled the term *transgender.* I was curious, that's all. After reading and rereading the Wikipedia definition a minimum of fifteen times, I translated it into plain English: Transgender people do not identity with their biological sex. Which causes many problems for many people.

There was a lot more info on the internet about transgender issues, like controversial bathroom laws and Caitlyn Jenner and crazy-high suicide rates and LGBTQ rights and Hormone Replacement Therapy. Maybe if I read an article a day, in ten years, I'll have a slight clue of what Julian/Julia is going through. Maybe I would, if I cared.

If I cared....

Despite the fact that this cafeteria pizza is the most promising meal in my near future, I lose my appetite. Getting up from the table, I say, "Gotta head." Only problem is, I have nowhere to go.

CHAPTER 19—THURSDAY

Julia, 7:00 p.m.

"HOW ARE you feeling, Julia? We haven't had a lot of time to talk since you started on the hormones."

Mama and I have met for tea at the Global Village Coffee Shop between her shifts at the senior center. It's nice to see her sitting down. She's been working even more hours since she knows I want to have some electrolysis done on my chin.

Last night before bed, I told her I could get a part-time job now that I'm not involved in all the after-school clubs, but instead of saying it was a great idea, she insisted I stay involved with my usual activities at Crestdale High School. I haven't yet decided if I want to return to the high school for extracurricular activities. I guess I'm scared. Who in my shoes wouldn't be? "I don't feel much different physically, but it's only been a few weeks. In my head, though…."

"What about 'in your head'?" Mama's gaze is laser-focused on my eyes. She's eager to hear that I'm somehow "better." And I *am* better, mostly because my outlook is radically improved.

"I feel sort of lighter in my mind." It's difficult to explain, but I have to try. "And hopeful… like I *care* about stuff more now. It's… it's as if a switch inside my head got flipped, and I'm… I'm *real* now… and I'm *finally living.*" The feeling I have is impossible to put into words, and I'm not sure if I'm ready to try. But my mother has sacrificed everything so I can have this indescribable experience, so I owe her my openness.

Mama smiles, and I do too. "Have you been in touch with Anna and Kandy?"

"Uh-huh. Every single day. We group text in the morning and at lunch, and they each call me at night. I'm gonna meet them for lunch on

Saturday at the mall." I don't consider them "volunteer friends" anymore. Anna and Kandy are just plain friends. "They want me to come back to school senior year, but I'm not ready to make that decision yet."

"They're good friends to you, Jules, as you are to them. And how about that boy you helped and his cousin who ran away? Have they kept in contact with you?"

I hate to burst her bubble, but I'm an honest girl and I promised Mama I wouldn't lie to her ever again. "No, I haven't heard a word from Hughie or Kale." I tuck a loose strand of hair into my bun, which I'll gladly never again refer to as a man bun. "I'm okay with it." I don't have much choice.

"If they can't handle the fact that you're transitioning, then you're probably better off without them."

I nod, but still, there's an inexplicable emptiness inside me. It's like I lost something that I never really had. "I didn't even tell Hughie I was gonna start online school. As far as he knows, I just dropped off the face of the earth."

"And what about Kale?" Mama pulls a peanut butter cookie out of the brown paper bag that the Global Village uses to package their bakery items, breaks it in half on a napkin, and pushes one part toward me. "Weren't you a little bit closer to him?"

"Kale knows I'm Julia now. He was at the human rights meeting last Friday night."

"And he had a negative reaction? I thought you said the group was supportive."

Mama looked calm for about three minutes, but now her anxiety is back, showing itself in worry lines on her forehead and in deep creases beside her mouth. She's worried I'm going to be assaulted, which is a legitimate concern for many people in my position, and their mothers.

"The group as a whole was supportive—awesomely so. But Kale... well, not so much."

"I hope you won't let one boy drive you away from an organization that needs you."

"And that *I* need...." But I get what she's saying.

"Maybe so. Don't let a single disapproving voice drive you away. Because, Jules, there are going to be *many* disapproving voices—many of them. And you need to brace your heart and your soul and your mind, and even your body, against them."

I know Mama's right, even if I wish so much she was mistaken. "I've chosen an unconventional path, haven't I?"

"You chose the only path you could follow. And now, my beautiful, smart, and courageous daughter, I hope you will follow it with pride." Mama's eyes are wet, but she isn't actually crying. I think she's more moved by how far we've come. "By the way, I got word from the insurance company that they're considering our request. I think we can be hopeful, but we shouldn't hold our breath."

"It's better than an outright rejection," I say.

"It most certainly is."

At the very same time, we both lift our heavy mugs of tea and click them together.

"To my daughter, Julia," Mama says, trying not to cry.

She fails.

CHAPTER 20—FRIDAY

Julia, 8:10 p.m.

I ARRIVE at REHO, as always, fashionably late, thanks to an extended meeting with Dr. Evelyn that went much better than I expected. We ended up talking right through dinnertime. Dr. Evelyn had a lot of deep and detailed questions, which at first I found annoying. A big part of me wants to get on with life as Julia and pull the plug on all of the analyzing and obsessing over the transition itself. But the more realistic part of me knows that counseling is going to guide me through what will be a very challenging, but hopefully positive, time in my life. So I opened up and spilled my guts. And spilled some more. By the end of our meeting, Dr. Evelyn couldn't shut me up.

Anyway, if Kale's going to come to the meeting, he'll be arriving fashionably *later* than me.

I glance down at my stylish ensemble of black leggings and a fuzzy pink sweater I got at a secondhand shop, with a lacy chalk-white tank poking out from underneath, and decide, *no one* can be more *fashionably* late than me. It just makes him a no-show.

The members, who are already in the circle, greet me with smiles, but they don't have even a second to actually say anything beyond hello, as Judy's about to start the pledge.

"We gather tonight in the spirit of love and selflessness, and with the solemn hope that our efforts to serve the community will be sufficient to keep hope alive for those who struggle to obtain the rights inherent to all human beings."

After reciting the pledge, Judy moves to the center of the circle. She hasn't made a move like this since I started attending REHO. Human beings are such creatures of habit; the slightest change in procedure is jarring. We all stare at her.

"It is easy to *say* that we are supporters of the rights of all human beings, but every once in a while, we are put to a test. Is this belief truly an integral part of our being? Can we own what we profess?" Judy looks around the circle, and I know she's noticed Kale isn't here tonight. "However, we need to be patient and encouraging as individuals discern whether the ability to truly accept the differences between us is within the grasp of their hearts and souls."

"Judy," says Karima softly, "I think it takes time to learn what sits comfortably with our consciences. Sometimes to learn this, we have to do something that doesn't sit well. And then we have to make the necessary changes."

"That was a perceptive remark, Karima. And so, people, if you have bared your soul and expressed your individuality and it was met with contention, *please understand* that this does not mean that you are not deserving of your rights, or that someone is trying to intentionally deprive you of them." Judy looks directly at me and says more softly, "Give Kale a little bit of time to adjust."

I nod and smile sweetly when I really want to shrug and say, "Maybe you should keep your cute little nose outta my private business, lady." The circle breaks apart to get the pillows out of the closet.

Karima hands me the purple one with a smile and says, "Go ahead and sit down, Julia."

I do as she suggests and soon the whole group is sitting around me.

"Let me tell you, young lady, I'm very impressed by your honesty and courage. Let me tell you...," says Billy.

"If you ever want to come over and bake a cake with me, dear, I'd love to have you," Tilly offers. I'm tempted to ask her what about me suggests I'd like to bake a freaking cake, but I don't because I recognize the offer as Tilly's flimsy way of letting me know she accepts my new gender role of "girl."

"I'm b-b-behind you, J-Julia, e-every st-step of the w-way," Tom informs me as he sits down a little bit too close in back of me. His knees press into my back.

"Now, people," starts Judy, from her spot in the front of the room. "Edna and Billy had the excellent idea of creating an adopt-a-grandparent program in our community. There are as many elderly people who feel lonely as there are children who feel neglected and…."

I don't mean to lose focus, but I'm completely distracted when Kale walks quietly from the bottom of the stairs and into the room, stopping about ten feet away from the group. He's dressed like he's been out running, holds a baseball cap in his hands, and stares at the floor in front of him. His short blond hair isn't quite so spiky, as it's grown in some. It now falls in soft curls against his head.

"Oh, Kale… I feared you wouldn't make it tonight. We are so glad you're here." Judy crosses the room and grabs a pillow out of the closet. She steps carefully in between all of the group members' spots on the floor and places the pillow right next to me. "Please, come sit down."

Kale doesn't look up but obediently walks over to the empty pillow with his ass's name on it and kneels down, then slides to the side. No Birkenstocks today, sneakers instead. And there's mud on them. I think he actually has been outside running. I never knew he was a runner. I guess there's a bunch of things we don't know about each other.

At first, he doesn't look at me, and I try my damnedest not to look at him either. Epic fail. Our gazes collide and there's a zing of connection in the air between us. We both quickly shift our gazes to the front of the room.

"And so, I would like us to plan the activities that the adopted grandparents will do with their adopted grandchildren. And I'd like a few volunteers to help Billy and Edna create a personality checklist that we will use to match the partners."

I hear what Judy is saying, but I'm honestly completely distracted by Kale. Maybe I'm sidetracked because he looks handsome in his sports attire. Maybe I'm troubled by the fact that I let him believe I was one thing, and I shocked him with the fact that I'm another. And maybe I did this knowing there was something beyond friendship growing between us. Maybe I feel guilty I didn't give Kale a heads-up on any of this that has made my mind unable to focus on adopted grandparents.

I don't slide closer to him to offer my explanation. I'm not sure how he feels about transgender people, and I honestly don't want to push my luck. I lean to the side just a little bit and say, "I should have given you a heads-up… you know, about this." I gesture to my outfit. "I'm sorry."

"No harm done," he replies without looking at me.

"Are you sure?"

He shrugs, and I know that some harm *was* definitely done. "You quit school?"

"I'm enrolled in online high school now."

"How are you going to be Crestdale's valedictorian when you don't even go to our high school anymore?"

It's my turn to shrug. "I guess other stuff was more important to me than graduating as number one."

"Like hiding?" This sounds dangerously close to an accusation.

"Like avoiding all the BS that would get slung at me in school from the kids who can't accept me as a girl."

Kale thinks about it for a second or two and then mumbles, "Yeah, I guess you have a point."

"Can *you* accept me as a girl?" I turn to study his face and I just know he isn't going to look at me, but he does. In his eyes, I see pain and confusion.

"I want to. You know, I want to accept you." He stops and swallows deeply, and then he coughs. After that, he makes a couple of hiccupping sounds, like he's putting off what he's about to reveal. "I'm just trying to understand what's going on with *me*… when it comes to *you*."

I nod once and say, "I get that."

Then we each get scooped up into separate activity planning groups, and that's all she wrote.

Kale, 9:30 p.m.

AFTER WE put the pillows back in the closet, I ask Julian/Julia, "Can I drive you home?" It doesn't hurt to ask. He can say yes or no.

But Julian/Julia doesn't answer with a simple yes or no. "Are you pissed off at me, Kale?" He looks up, challenging me with pretty painted eyes.

But there's more than mere *challenge* in his eyes. When Julia/Julian looks at me, it's as if he's sizing me up, or maybe conducting some sort of a safety check. It hits me hard when I realize he's trying to assure himself that I'm not going to kick the crap out of him as soon as I get him alone. Because he's a transgender girl and I'm an asshole. "Don't worry, Julian, you're safe with me."

"Julia. My name is Julia." I get that sizing-up look again.

It's obvious that I need to stop thinking of him as *him* and I need to start thinking of him as *her*. *Of her as her.* And I'm going to start right now. "Sorry, Julia."

She smiles and *her* lips are as pretty as Julian's lips. Full and shiny and... I'm suddenly confused again.

"I'm gonna go grab my coat." I watch her as she floats back to where she was sitting and picks up her black trench coat from the floor.

Edna and Tilly smile as we walk together toward the stairs. Edna says, "Have a nice night, kids." Tilly grins, and I swear she's about to add something like, "Don't do anything I wouldn't do," but she resists and I'm incredibly thankful.

We walk in silence to Dad's Cube. I decide to be polite, so I unlock her door and open it, but *shit, this is weird!*

"Thanks, Kale." She smiles and I know it isn't weird for her. It works very well for Julia.

I walk around the car slowly, trying to get my head together. I have no idea what I want to say to her, or even what I'm doing here with her. As I slide into the driver seat, I issue the world's stupidest demand. "Buckle up for safety."

Shoot me now....

Julia nods and buckles up. We pull onto the street and there's more silence.

After a few minutes, she says in a soft voice, "I know this must be really messed-up for you."

I don't nod or shrug or shake my head. I glance at her, though, and she's looking straight ahead, so I turn back to the road and just drive. It's the easiest thing for me to do.

144

At least a full minute passes before she speaks again. "This has been a very long time coming for me."

The new honest Kale replies, "I'm starting to get that."

Kale, 9:45 p.m.

I PARK outside the coffee shop but don't shut off the engine. This isn't a date. And we aren't really friends. I don't know what we are, just like I don't know who I am. Until we figure this stuff out, I'm going to have to be okay with uncertainty.

"Want to have a cup of coffee and talk for a while? My treat," she offers. Her voice is so thin, just a little more than a whisper.

I shake my head. "Not tonight."

"Well, thanks for the ride. You saved me a lot of money on a taxi, seeing as I'm not quite ready to ride the bus yet." Julia turns from me and starts to get out of the car.

"Wait."

She glances at me over her shoulder. "Wait for what?"

I sit here like a dork and stare at her chin. I'm not sure why it's her chin I choose to stare at. I guess it feels like a safe zone. I won't get too emotional if I concentrate my gaze on her chin... or her nose, maybe, if the chin stops working.

"You already told me you don't want to have coffee and talk. So you must want to get the hell outta here." Julia sits back down and her pretty dark hair falls against the headrest. "Look, Kale. There's no need for you to feel bad, or to drive me home, or to be my friend. I'm not pissed off at you for being uncomfortable with me. It is what it is. No worries."

I stay 100 percent focused on the chin. It's a fine chin. Slightly sharp—like her personality.

"Okay?" she prods.

"Julia." This is her name. *Her name.* "I'm so selfish. I made you... and your transition... your being a girl, all about me."

145

"I don't get what you're trying to say. I'm the one who's changing, so how can this be about you?"

My gaze is pulled away from her chin and is dragged up to her eyes. "You look as confused as I feel," I offer.

"Why are *you* confused? You're a guy—inside and out. That's not confusing." Her retort is as pointed as her chin.

I have no idea why I want her to understand my feelings. Maybe I want her help, even if I have no right to it. "Julia, it's not my gender that confuses me. It's… it's not so easy to explain."

"Believe me, I understand that. But try me."

I decide I'm going to go for it—complete and unbridled honesty. I did it with Dad; I did it with Hughie. I can do it with Julia too. "What confuses me, is… is how I feel about *you*."

Her eyes widen. They look even prettier than before. I want to pull out my phone and take a picture so I can remember her expression.

"So maybe I thought I was… sort of gay, because I *liked* you, you know, when you were a boy."

Slowly, Julia shakes her head.

"I was shocked to shit when I found out you were gonna be… that you *are* a girl." I run my fingers over my head, expecting to feel dreadlocks, and am surprised that I just feel hair. "And even when I was shocked, and maybe a little bit angry that you didn't give me a hint this was coming, I still sort of *liked* you. *That way*, you know? How am I supposed to explain *that*?"

Julia stops shaking her head and smiles. "I think you might just like the me-ness of me."

"The you-ness of you?"

She nods. "You're attracted to a certain quality in me, rather than my gender. And I think that's pretty cool."

"It is? I mean, you do?" I'm worse than a dork. I'm a loser. I probably should have kept my mouth shut. But I didn't; I told the truth. And judging from the gentle expression in her eyes, she isn't laughing at me.

"For some people, Kale, it's not all about gender."

I'm not 100 percent sure that she's right, but I'm not sure she's wrong, either. I decide to let the subject go, and I blurt out the question that's on my mind. "Are you still allowed to be a part of the Gay-Straight Alliance at Crestdale High School?"

"The principal decided that I'd be able to continue with my clubs at Crestdale High, but I haven't made up my mind if I want to do that yet."

"If you decide to be in GSA, I'll sit with you, okay?" My offer is lame, but I hope she gets my drift. I'm going to have her back. It might be hard, but not as hard as what *she's* doing.

"I'll think about it, Kale."

"So, I hope I'll see you Wednesday afternoon." This is as good a place to say goodbye as any. We both have some thinking to do.

CHAPTER 21—WEDNESDAY

Julia, 3:00 p.m.

I'VE GOT Anna on my right side and Kandy on my left. They're actually holding on to my arms to give me support. Hughie and Kale are meeting us in the science classroom. *This is going to be okay.*

"Hughie joined GSA to support you? That's so sweet and thoughtful," Anna says.

"I never thought of Hughie as *sweet* before, but I'm willing to go with it," I reply, trying to keep a straight face.

They giggle and Kandy squeezes my arm. "This is going to work out just fine—don't you worry." I wish I had her confidence.

When we get to the classroom, Hughie and Kale wave at us. We sit down with them, and our little group fits together perfectly. So far, I feel relatively safe at Crestdale High School as Julia Mendez. And Mama emailed Ms. Valencia, letting her know that I'd be attending today and that I didn't want to be singled out in any way.

We work together as a small group on bullying intervention scenarios, and although I notice some of the other kids in GSA looking at me curiously, they flash shaky smiles when I catch them.

After the meeting, I walk with Hughie and Kale across the parking lot toward Kale's mother's minivan. I'm feeling a little bit giddy because I'd never thought it would happen like this. I became Julia, and although I felt I had to withdraw from public school, I think I can still participate in at least some of my after-school activities. And I have friends—more friends than I had when I was Julian—and I have a crush on a guy who might like me too, which remains to be seen, and I'm not planning on holding my breath. But still….

Kale slows down so that Hughie is walking a few steps in front of us, and he pushes up against my side. "I like your blouse. You know, the silkiness of it. And the color yellow too."

He likes my blouse because it's silky and yellow? I think he's trying to say he's cool with *me*. "Thanks, Kale. Your shirt rocks too. Purple is one of my favorite colors."

"It's fruit juice tie-dyed—blueberry juice to be exact. I dyed it myself."

"Way cool."

"Anyhow, I thought maybe we could drop Hughie off and then grab some food at the Carriway Pancake House."

"Sounds great, but I'm broke today."

"My treat." He reaches out and touches my arm. I'm so stunned that I stop walking and stare at him. "I want to take you to dinner."

"Um… that sounds perfect, Kale. And I'm in the mood for pancakes. I mean isn't everybody pretty much *always* in the mood for pancakes?" I'm rambling. There's a first time for everything, and *nervous rambling* happened sooner for me as Julia than I'd expected. But I don't really care and so I smile anyway.

Kale, 4:30 p.m.

"HEY, CRUNCHY, what're ya doing with the she-male?" It's Robbie—just the person I didn't want to bump into—and he's with a girl. They're laughing like something is hilarious.

"Get lost, Rob." I say it with the most badass tone I can muster, but we both know Robbie is the tough guy here. Thanks to all of the nonsalad he eats, the guy is twice my size. I glance briefly at Julia. Her smile is history.

"So, Oswald, you're not a save-the-earth, super-crunchy dude no more, and *now* you're into girly-boys? What's goin' on with ya, huh?" Robbie asks.

Then it's the girl's turn. She squints and launches her verbal attack. "*Julia,* did you know that your freaky boyfriend used to be one of those dirty-ass, earthy dudes? These two oddballs fit together perfectly, if you ask me."

Nobody asked, I think but keep my mouth shut.

"Kale Oswald was about as crunchy as they come, Sydney. It's why he's so skinny—no meat for months." Robbie shakes his head, probably still wondering why the heck I won't make a meal out of living beings with faces.

The girl looks me up and down. "Skin and bones is right."

"Hey, Crunchy! I thought you were driving us home. Let's go!" Hughie's leaning on my mother's minivan. If this girl is Sydney Harper, the nasty one in all his classes that he told me about, it's no wonder he hasn't come any closer to us. She really gets under his skin.

"Look, Kale, me and Sydney are gonna hang out at the arcade for a few and then hit the library. Come on along. Leave the losers in your dust."

"I can't today. I'm driving my friend and my cousin home." Again, I glance at Julia. She looks scared. And truthfully, I'm scared too, because I know if Robbie wants to, he can kick my butt to the moon. And then kick Julia and Hughie's butts to Venus and Mars. But at the same time I'm scared, I'm feeling kind of fierce. Weird.

"Let Hugh-ball drive *it* home. Go ahead, Oswald, toss him the keys—Hugh hasn't got anything better to do, and we all know it." Robbie still appears genuinely confused about why I won't cut and run on a couple of "losers."

"I have a better idea—you go your way and I'll go mine." I mean it.

"You sayin' ya *wanna* go with *that thing*?" He jabs a finger at Julia, and I step between them. I'm no hero—it's more or less an instinct to protect Hughie and Julia because they don't deserve more bad luck.

Robbie always thought I was just like him. And I went along with it for way too long, but still I had a feeling I was different from him. I tried my best to be a hippie, but I failed miserably. And I'll admit that I'm probably one of the least selfless human rights activists in REHO history. But I'm changing.

I guess the question here is: Can I live with myself if I toss the minivan keys to Hughie and head off to the arcade with Robbie and Sydney? And maybe a better question is: Do I even *want* to leave Hughie and Julia in favor of spending time with Robbie and Sydney?

"Sorry, Robbie, but I don't fear ridicule and retribution enough to go with you guys."

"Huh?" Robbie isn't the sharpest tool in the shed, and my meaning is clearly lost on him.

So I translate it into words Robbie will understand. "You know what? I've already got plans. I'm going to drop Hughie off at home and then I'm taking Julia out for pancakes."

"What are you, some kind of faggot, Oswald?" Robbie's mad, and when he's mad, things can get ugly.

Smart enough to resist the urge to throw back another insult, I decide to interpret Robbie's surge of hostility as our cue to leave. "Let's go, Julia."

Dad once told me to never turn my back on a big cat. Since there aren't many lions and tigers roaming around Crestdale, I banished this advice to the back of my mind. Right now I realize that I *completely* missed my father's message. Because the second I turn my back on Robbie, he's pretty much on top of me, dragging me down to the ground, and it's not thumb wrestling he has in mind. I've never before exchanged so much as heated words with another guy, so needless to say I'm an inexperienced fighter. I flail my arms in a futile attempt to distract him. Robbie only has time to punch me once in the jaw and a second time in the gut before Julia and Hughie pull him off me.

Thankfully, Sydney is about as interested in being involved in a fight on school grounds as I am. "God, Robbie, way to get yourself suspended. And I'm not going down with you, so make a choice—it's either me and the arcade or some loser who's named after cabbage and his freaky misfit pals. I don't take time away from studying to get myself kicked out of school."

Robbie brushes the sand off his hands and knees. "Since ya put it that way, it's easy. We're *so* outta here, Sydney." And off they go on their merry, bullying way. My relief is intense.

I can't stand up straight, as it feels like Robbie's meaty fist is *still* lodged in my gut. I manage to murmur, "I think I'm going to have to find someone else to sit with at lunch."

Hughie comes over to me and dusts the gravel off my back. "I'd say it's way past time for that."

The laughter hurts my jaw, but it's worth it because I stuck it out with my friends instead of ditching them to keep my social standing. I'm sure I'll pay a heavy price for it at school, but sometimes you've got to risk it all and do the right thing. Maybe my gut and jaw are throbbing, but everything else about me feels pretty good.

"I figured it would have been *me* they'd have come after," Julia says quietly. Her eyes are wide, and I wonder if it's with a sense of relief or disbelief. "I mean, seriously, I'm a freaking target, and the asshole went after you."

"You put yourself out there for us, Crunchy. Now we owe you our lives." Hughie is pretty witty when you take the time to listen to him. "I'll drive, and you can stretch out in the back seat."

"Maybe pancakes should wait until another night, when it won't hurt you so much to chew," Julia says, and she actually looks disappointed.

Inside I cheer, and then I agree. "How about we do it Saturday night instead? And maybe a movie after." Even injured, I attempt to seal the deal with Julia.

"It sounds like a plan, Kale." Those eyes flash and those lips curve into a smile and I swear that cute chin has a little dimple I never before noticed.

"It sounds like a *date*," Hughie murmurs as we get into the van.

Chapter 22 — Saturday

Julia, 7:00 p.m.

"So will she peel it off her face and then actually *eat* it?" I ask.

"I don't know if she *will*, but she *could* if she wanted to," Kale replies.

He has the use of his mother's minivan tonight because Mrs. Oswald is spending the evening at home with her husband and nephew, experimenting on *their* faces with do-it-yourself edible facials. According to Kale, she conducted an intense online search and decided upon a new career in all-natural skin care.

"Dad finally came clean with Mom about his concern over the lack of 'quality and quantity time' our family's been spending together. Mom actually heard what he had to say and decided to start a family skin-care business."

"That's so cool." Tonight, according to Kale, Mr. Oswald and Hughie are apparently being rewarded for his honesty with the bonding experience of DIY edible family facials.

"Before I left she was spooning squished-up bananas into a bowl of honey, Greek yogurt, and crushed pistachios. So in a way, Mom is cooking, which she never does, *and* hanging out with Dad and Hughie at the same time as she's moving forward with her new business."

"But crushed pistachios? Ouch."

"She said the nuts would slough away dead skin cells." This seems to make perfect sense to Kale.

"Oh. It might actually work, and I guess it could be tasty—but on my face, and *then* in my mouth... *ewwww*."

"Well, you don't need a facial. Your skin is... it's pretty much perfect."

I know I'm blushing, and strangely I'm okay with it. "Thanks, Kale. But still, sorry I made you miss an opportunity for family bonding." I smirk so he knows I'm joking.

"Don't be sorry. I'm fine with missing it—I have a feeling there'll be plenty more chances to bond, because we're all committed to getting Oswald's Face Paste and More, Ltd. off the ground. And, just saying, if I'm going to eat honey-drizzled bananas, they're gonna be sliced up and served on my pancakes." Kale pulls the minivan into a spot at the far end of the Carriway Pancake House parking lot. He leaves the engine running, so I think maybe he wants to talk.

"Mmmm… sounds tempting. Maybe I'll have pancakes with a few slices of crunchy bacon." He looks at me strangely when I mention bacon, but then he smiles.

I'm on my very first date, not that dating was something I'd planned on at this point in my transition. Okay, maybe dating was about the last thing on my mind. All I wanted was to live as a girl. To freely *be* the girl I am. And it's happening. So my first date with a cute guy I actually like is a total bonus.

Kale suddenly looks worried. "What's wrong?" I ask, hoping he'll be as honest with me as his dad's been with his mom.

"I still feel like I owe you an explanation for the way I acted when you came out as Julia."

I shake my head. "I get that you were shocked, Kale. And people act in all different ways when their minds have been blown."

"But the way I went crazy—it wasn't as much about you as it was about me. I think what freaked me out most about your change was that I liked you *that way* when I thought you were a gay guy *and* as a straight girl." He still looks confused.

"I don't know if gender is necessarily the most important thing in every relationship. Don't you think you could just like something about me? Not me the guy or me the girl… just me the person."

"Yeah, I think so. I googled it." Kale is fair-skinned and I can't miss the way he's turning red. "I typed in the search bar 'I like a transgender girl' and I found lots of stories about other guys who are interested in transgender girls. I read for like three hours."

It's clear to me that Kale's working through a confusing mental scenario, and he just so happens to be doing it out loud, in the driver seat of his mother's minivan, on our first date.

"I guess I like to put stuff in categories, and once I found out there was a category for *me*, I could calm down." Kale finally stops the engine, unbuckles, and turns to face me. "And I think I still want to be an activist, even if I'm not so much a hippie anymore."

"What kind of an activist?" The cold air from outside pushes its way into the warmth of the car, but still I'm in no hurry to leave. This is important.

"Probably I'll be an activist for lots of things to do with human rights. See, in every fight somebody has got to be on the front line—I think *I* want to be there, breaking down the barriers," he says.

My heart skips a beat. "So REHO is the right organization for you?"

"I think so. Maybe you *are* out on the front line, Julia, but you aren't out there alone."

He smiles, and I melt. Then I shiver.

"I think I'd like to kiss you before we freeze to death."

I'm in shock because Kale has changed so much in a few weeks. It's like he grew up, or got a clue, or maybe he saw the light. I thought all transitions took years to happen, but I guess when you're ready to have any kind of growth spurt, even one in your mind, time isn't a factor.

"Well, what're you waiting for?" I ask.

That's all the invitation Kale needs. He leans toward me, takes my hand, and gives Julia Mendez her first kiss ever. This time when I shiver, it's not because I'm cold and it's not because I'm scared.

It's a thrilling-first-kiss kind of shiver, and what girl wouldn't like that?

MIA KERICK is the mother of four exceptional children—one in law school, another at a dance conservatory, a third studying at Mia's alma mater, Boston College, and her lone son still in high school. She has published more than twenty books of LGBTQ romance when not editing National Honor Society essays, offering opinions on college and law school applications, helping to create dance bios, and reviewing English papers. Her husband of twenty-five years has been told by many that he has the patience of Job, but don't ask Mia about this, as it is a sensitive subject.

Mia focuses her stories on the emotional growth of troubled young people and their relationships. She has a great affinity for the tortured hero. There is, at minimum, one in each book. As a teen, Mia filled spiral-bound notebooks with tales of said tortured heroes (most of whom happened to strongly resemble lead vocalists of 1980s hair bands) and stuffed them under her mattress for safekeeping. She is thankful to Harmony Ink Press for providing her with an alternate place to stash her stories.

Her books have won several positive Kirkus Book Reviews that were selected for Kirkus Reviews magazine, a Best YA Lesbian Rainbow Award, a Best Transgender Contemporary Romance Rainbow Award, Reader Views' Book by Book Publicity Literary Award, the Jack Eadon Award for Best Book in Contemporary Drama, an Indie Fab Award, and a Royal Dragonfly Award for Cultural Diversity, among other awards.

Mia Kerick is a social liberal and cheers for each and every victory made in the name of human rights. Her only major regret: never having taken typing or computer class in school, destining her to a life consumed with two-fingered pecking and constant prayer to the Gods of Technology. Contact Mia at miakerick@gmail.com or visit at www.miakerickya.com to see what is going on in Mia's world.

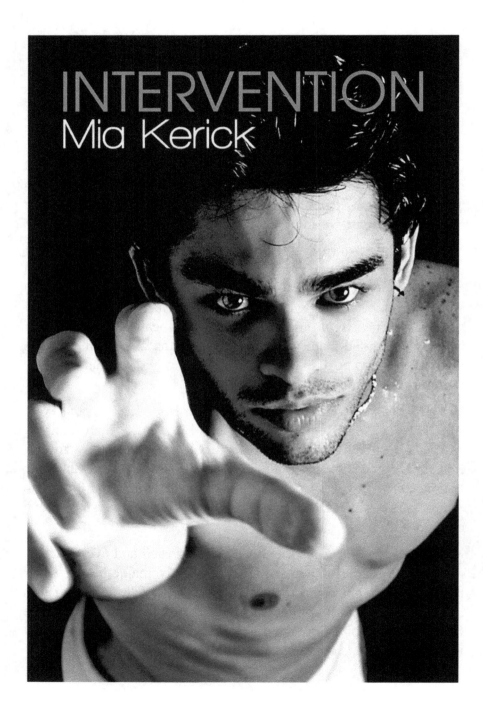

INTERVENTION
Mia Kerick

As a musician at the popular college café Coed Joe's, high school senior Kai Manter is never lacking for male attention. Out, proud, free-spirited, and sexually aware, Kai sets his sights on his darkly Gothic and undeniably bad-tempered coworker, Jamie Arlotta, a freshman at the local arts university. Sporting long hair and alluring hippie style, Kai expects his interest will be reciprocated, with satisfying sex as the end goal. That's what usually happens. But Jamie's lessons in life have been harsher. Having been sexually abused by his older stepbrother for several years, Jamie has grown an impenetrable outer shell meant to keep the world at a safe distance.

Kai is angry at first when he takes the brunt of Jamie's bad temper, but after Kai accidentally discovers the abuse Jamie has suffered, he wants to fix things. Kai's plan is based on what he knows best—music—and he stages a "musical intervention" to let Jamie know he's not alone and things can get better. When Jamie's perspective changes and he emerges from his shell, Kai changes, too, gaining a whole new understanding of what sex can be when love is there too.

www.harmonyinkpress.com

NOT BROKEN,
JUST BENT

MIA KERICK

Braving the start of high school, longtime childhood friends Benjamin Wells and Timmy Norton quickly realize they are entering a whole new world colored by their family responsibilities. Ben is trying to please his strict father; Timmy is taking care of his younger sisters. While their easy camaraderie is still comfortable, Ben notices Timmy growing distant and evasive, but Ben has his own problems. It's easier to let concerns about Timmy's home life slide, especially when Timmy changes directions and starts to get a little too close. Ben doesn't know how to handle the new feelings Timmy's desire for love inspires, and his continuing denial wounds Timmy deeply.

But what Timmy perceives as Ben's greatest betrayal is yet to come, and the fallout threatens to break them apart forever. Over the next four years, the push and pull between them and the outside world twists and tears at Ben and Timmy, and they are haunted by fear and regret. However, sometimes what seems broken is just a little bent, and if they can find forgiveness within themselves, Ben and Timmy may be able to move forward together.

www.harmonyinkpress.com

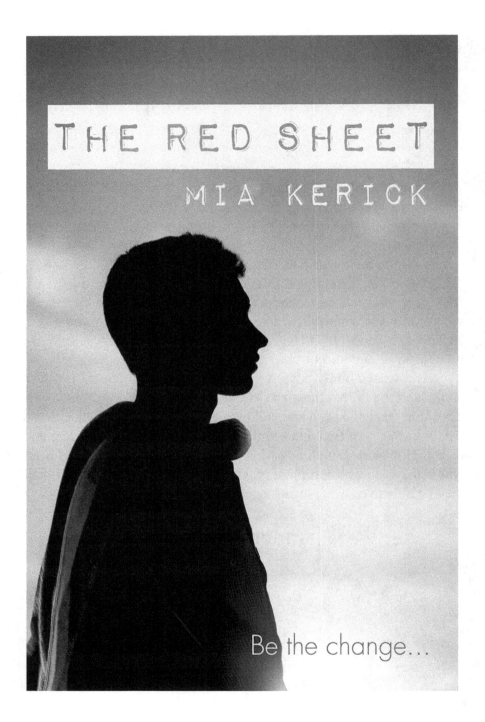

THE RED SHEET

MIA KERICK

Be the change...

One October morning, high school junior Bryan Dennison wakes up a different person—helpful, generous, and chivalrous—a person whose new admirable qualities he doesn't recognize. Stranger still is the urge to tie a red sheet around his neck like a cape.

Bryan soon realizes this compulsion to wear a red cape is accompanied by more unusual behavior. He can't hold back from retrieving kittens from tall trees, helping little old ladies cross busy streets, and defending innocence anywhere he finds it.

Shockingly, at school, he realizes he used to be a bully. He's attracted to the former victim of his bullying, Scott Beckett, though he has no memory of Scott from before "the change." Where he'd been lazy in academics, overly aggressive in sports, and socially insecure, he's a new person. And although he can recall behaving egotistically, he cannot remember his motivations.

Everyone, from his mother to his teachers to his "superjock" former pals, is shocked by his dramatic transformation. However, Scott Beckett is not impressed by Bryan's newfound virtue. And convincing Scott he's genuinely changed and improved, hopefully gaining Scott's trust and maybe even his love, becomes Bryan's obsession.

www.harmonyinpkress.com

Renzy Callen exists on the periphery of life, and not just because of the horrific childhood event that robbed him of the ability to speak. Walling himself off from the rest of the world as a means of protection, he occupies his time with art, music, and an obsession with self-help groups—whether he needs them or not. His isolation protects him, and he's immune to drama and emotional games… or so he believes. Everything changes when he meets Seven and Morning Moreaux-Maddox, the wealthy, jet-setting siblings who move from a life of sophistication in Europe to humdrum Redcliff Hills, Missouri.

Both Seven and his sister are impossibly beautiful and elegant, like the stars in magazines and high-fashion models on the runway. When Renzy is pulled into their push-and-pull of affection and rejection, he realizes there is more to both haunted Morning and cold, diamond-sharp Seven than meets the eye.

The three teens embark on a quest to learn the reason behind Renzy's selective mutism, and something more than friendship blossoms between Renzy and Seven. It's during this trip of a lifetime that the three realize the truth they seek might be found in the sound of silence.

www.harmonyinkpress.com

US
THREE

Mia Kerick

One Voice: Book One

In his junior year at a public high school, sweet, bright Casey Minton's biggest worry isn't being gay. Keeping from being too badly bullied by his so-called friends, a group of girls called the Queen Bees, is more pressing. Nate De Marco has no friends, his tough home life having taken its toll on his reputation, but he's determined to get through high school. Zander Zane's story is different: he's popular, a jock. Zander knows he's gay, but fellow students don't, and he'd like to keep it that way.

No one expects much when these three are grouped together for a class project, yet in the process the boys discover each other's talents and traits, and a new bond forms. But what if Nate, Zander, and Casey fall in love—each with the other and all three together? Not only gay but also a threesome, for them high school becomes infinitely more complicated and maybe even dangerous. To survive and keep their love alive, they must find their individual strengths and courage and stand together, honest and united. If they can do that, they might prevail against the Queen Bees and a student body frightened into silence—and even against their own crippling fears.

www.harmonyinkpress.com

Mick & Michelle

NINA ROSSING

CPSIA information can be obtained
at www.ICGtesting.com
Printed in the USA
LVHW01s0914221018
594370LV00022B/1123/P

9 781640 803930